The Story of 1

An Historical Romance

Alfred Henry Lewis

Alpha Editions

This edition published in 2024

ISBN : 9789362920546

Design and Setting By
Alpha Editions
www.alphaedis.com
Email - info@alphaedis.com

As per information held with us this book is in Public Domain.
This book is a reproduction of an important historical work. Alpha Editions uses the best technology to reproduce historical work in the same manner it was first published to preserve its original nature. Any marks or number seen are left intentionally to preserve its true form.

Contents

CHAPTER I HIS BAPTISM OF THE SEA .... - 1 -

CHAPTER II IN THE BLACK TRADE .... - 5 -

CHAPTER III THE YELLOW JACK .... - 12 -

CHAPTER IV THE KILLING OF MUNGO .... - 20 -

CHAPTER V THE SAILOR TURNS PLANTER .... - 24 -

CHAPTER VI THE FIRST BLOW IN VIRGINIA .... - 28 -

CHAPTER VII THE BLAST OF WAR .... - 33 -

CHAPTER VIII THE PLANTER TURNS LIEUTENANT .... - 39 -

CHAPTER IX THE CRUISE OF THE "PROVIDENCE" .... - 45 -

CHAPTER X THE COUNSEL OF CADWALADER .... - 48 -

CHAPTER XI THE GOOD SHIP RANGER .... - 54 -

CHAPTER XII HOW THE "RANGER" TOOK THE "DRAKE" .... - 60 -

CHAPTER XIII THE DUCHESS OF CHARTRES .... - 66 -

CHAPTER XIV THE SAILING OF THE "RICHARD" .... - 73 -

CHAPTER XV THE "RICHARD" AND THE "SERAPIS" .... - 80 -

CHAPTER XVI HOW THE BATTLE RAGED .... - 85 -

CHAPTER XVII THE SURRENDER OF THE "SERAPIS" .... - 90 -

CHAPTER XVIII DIPLOMACY AND THE DUTCH .... - 95 -

CHAPTER XIX NOW FOR THE TRAITOR LANDAIS .... - 99 -

CHAPTER XX AIMEE ADELE DE TELISON .... - 104 -

CHAPTER XXI ANTONY AND CLEOPATRA .... - 106 -

CHAPTER XXII THE FÊTE OF THE DUCHESS DE CHARTRES .... - 110 -

CHAPTER XXIII THE WEDDING WITHOUT BELLS .... - 114 -

CHAPTER XXIV THAT HONEYMOON SUB ROSA .... - 118 -

CHAPTER XXV CATHERINE OF RUSSIA .... - 121 -

CHAPTER XXVI AN ADMIRAL OF RUSSIA .... - 124 -

CHAPTER XXVII THE HOUSE IN THE
RUE TOURNON ....- 126 -

CHAPTER XXVIII LOVE AND THOSE
LAST DAYS ....- 131 -

THE END ....- 134 -

CHAPTER I
HIS BAPTISM OF THE SEA

This is in the long-ago, or, to be exact, in July, 1759. The new brig Friendship, not a fortnight off the stocks, is lying in her home harbor of Whitehaven, being fitted to her first suit of sails. Captain Bennison is restlessly about her decks, overseeing those sea-tailors, the sail-makers, as they go forward with their task, when Mr. Younger, the owner, comes aboard. The latter gentleman is lowland Scotch, stout, middle-aged, and his severe expanse of smooth-shaven upper-lip tells of prudence, perseverance and Presbyterianism in even parts, as traits dominant of his character.

"Dick," says Mr. Younger, addressing Captain Bennison, "ye'll have a gude brig; and mon! ye s'uld have a gude crew. There'll be none of the last in Whitehaven, for what ones the agents showed me were the mere riff-raff of the sea. I'll even go to Arbigland, and pick ye a crew among the fisher people."

"Arbigland!" repeats Captain Bennison, with a glow of approval. "The Arbigland men are the best sailor-folk that ever saw the Solway. Give me an Arbigland crew, James, and I'll find ye the Rappahannock with the Friendship, within the month after she tears her anchor out o' Whitehaven mud."

And so Mr. Younger goes over to Arbigland.

It is a blowing July afternoon. An off-shore breeze, now freshening to a gale, tosses the Solway into choppy billows. Most of the inhabitants of Arbigland are down at the mouth of the little tide-water creek, that forms the harbor of the village, eagerly watching a small fishing yawl. The latter craft is beating up in the teeth of the gale, striving for the shelter of the creek.

The crew of the yawl consists of but one, and him a lad of twelve. His right hand holds the tiller; with the left he slacks or hauls the sheets, and shifts the sail when he goes about.

The yawl has just heeled over on the starboard tack, as Mr. Younger pushes in among the villagers that crowd the little quay.

"They'll no make it!" exclaims a fisherman, alluding to the boy and yawl; "they'll be blawn oot t' sea!"

"Ay! they'll make it sure enough," declares another stoutly. "It's little Jack Paul who's conning her, and he'd bring the yawl in against a horrycane. She's a gude boat, too—as quick on her feet as a dancing maister; and, as for beating to wind'ard, she'll lay a point closer to the wind than a man has a right to ask of his lawful wedded wife. Ye'll see; little Jack'll bring her in."

"Who is he?" asks Mr. Younger of the last speaker; "who's yon boy?"

"He's son to John Paul, gardener to the laird Craik."

"Sitha! son to Gardener Paul, quo' you!" breaks in an old fish-wife who, with red arms folded beneath her coarse apron, stands watching the yawl with the others. "Now to my mind, he looks mair like the laird than I s'uld want my son to look, if I were wife to Gardener Paul."

"Shame for ye, Lucky!" cries the fisherman to whom she speaks. "Would ye cast doots on the lad's mither, and only because the lad in his favoring makes ye think now and again on Maister Craik? Jeanny Paul, that was Jeanny Macduff, is well kenned to be as carefu' a wife as ever cooked her man's breakfast in Arbigland."

"Ye think so, Tam Bryce?" retorts the incorrigible Lucky. "Much ye s'uld know of the wives of Arbigland, and you to sea eleven months o' the year! I tell ye, Jeanny came fro' the Highlands; and it'll be lang, I trow, since gude in shape of man or woman came oot o' the Highlands."

"Guide your tongue, Lucky!" remonstrates the other, in a low tone; "guide your tongue, ye jade! Here comes Gardener Paul himsel'."

"I'll no stay to meet him," says Lucky, moving away. "Puir blinded fule! not to see what all Arbigland, ay! and all Kirkbean Parish, too, for that matter, has seen the twal years, that his boy Jack is no mair no less than just the laird's bairn when all's said."

"Ye'll no mind her, Maister Younger," says Tom Bryce, pointing after Lucky; "although, to be preceese, what the carline tells has in it mair of truth than poetry."

"I was no thinking on the dame's clack," returns Mr. Younger, his eyes still on the nearing yawl, "or whether yon lad's a gardener's bairn or a gentleman's by-blaw. What I will say, in the face of the sun, however, is that he has in him the rudiments of as brisk a sailorman as ever walked saut water."

"There'll be none that's better," observes Tom Bryce, "going in and oot o' Solway Firth." Then, eyeing the yawl: "He'll win to the creek's mouth on the next reach to sta'board."

Gardener Paul joins Mr. Younger and the fisherman, Tom Bryce.

"We were talking of your son," says Mr. Younger to Gardener Paul. "What say ye, mon; will ye apprentice him? I'll send him with Dick Bennison, in my new brig Friendship, to the Virginias and Jamaica."

John Paul, gardener to the laird, Robert Craik, is a dull man, notably thick of wit, and slow.

"The Virginias!" he repeats. "My son William has been there these sixteen year. He's head man for my kinsman Jones, on his plantation by the Rappahannock. If Jack sails with Dick Bennison, he'll meet William that he's never seen."

"He'll see his brother for sure," returns Mr. Younger. "The Friendship goes from Whitehaven to Urbana, and that's not a dozen miles down the Rappahannock from your cousin's plantation."

The yawl has come safely into the creek's mouth, and lies rocking at her moorings as lightly as a gull. The lad leaps ashore, and is patted on the back by the fisherman in praise of his seamanship. He smiles through the salt water that drips from his face; for beating to windward is not the driest point of sailing, and the lad is spray-soaked from head to heel.

"And may I go, father?"

"This is Mr. Younger, Jack," says Gardener Paul, as the lad conies up. "He wants ye to sail 'prentice with Dick Bennison, in the new brig." The difference to show between Gardener Paul and little Jack Paul, as the pair stand together on the quay, goes far to justify those innuendoes of the scandalous Lucky. Gardener Paul's heavy peasant face possesses nothing to mark, on his part, any blood-nearness to the boy, whose olive skin, large brown eyes, clean profile and dark hair like silk, speak only of the patrician.

"And may I go, father?" asks Jack, a flush breaking eagerly through the tan on his cheek.

"And may I go, father?"
Page 13.

"Ye might as weel, I think," responds Gardener Paul judgmatically. "Ye're the born petrel; and for the matter of gardening, being my own and Adam's trade, I've kenned for lang ye'll no mair touch spade or mattock than handle coals of fire. So, as I was saying, ye might as weel sail 'prentice with Dick; and when ye meet your brother William, gi' him his father's gude word. Ye'll never have seen William, Jack, for he left hame before ye were born; and so it'll be a braw fore-gathering between the twa of ye—being brothers that never met before."

And after this fashion the fisher-boy, John Panl, afterward Admiral Paul Jones, is given his baptism of the sea.

CHAPTER II
IN THE BLACK TRADE

The sun is struggling through the dust-coated, cobwebbed windows, and lighting dimly yet sufficiently the dingy office of Shipowner Younger of Whitehaven. That substantial man is sitting at his desk, eyes fixed upon the bristle of upstanding masts which sprout, thick as forest pines on a hillside, from the harbor basin below. The face of Shipowner Younger has been given the seasoning of several years, since he went to Arbigland that squall-torn afternoon, to pick up a crew for Dick Bennison. Also, Shipowner Younger shines with a new expression of high yet retiring complacency. The expression is one awful and fascinating to the clerk, who sits at the far end of the room. Shipowner Younger has been elected to Parliament, and his awful complacency is that elevation's visible sign. The knowledge of his master's election offers the basis of much of the clerk's awe, and that stipendary almost charms himself into the delusion that he sees a halo about the bald pate of Shipowner Younger.

The latter brings the spellbound clerk from his trance of fascination, by wheeling upon him.

"Did ye send doon, mon," he cries, "to my wharf, with word for young Jack Paul to come?"

The clerk says that he did.

"Then ye can go seek your denner."

The clerk, acting on this permission, scrambles to his fascinated feet. As he retires through the one door, young Jack Paul enters. The brown-faced boy of the Arbigland yawl has grown to be a brisk young sailor, taut and natty. He shakes the hand of Shipowner Younger, who gives him two fingers in that manner of condescending reserve, which he conceives to be due his dignity as a member of the House of Commons. Having done so much for his dignity, Shipowner Younger relaxes.

"Have a chair, lad!" he says. "Bring her here where we can chat."

The natty Jack Paul brings the clerk's chair, as being the only one in the room other than that occupied by Shipowner Younger. One sees the thorough-paced sailor in the very motions of him; for his step is quick, catlike and sure, and there is just the specter of a roll in his walk, as though the heaving swell of the ocean still abides in his heels. When he has placed the chair, so as to bring himself and Shipowner Younger face to face, he says:

"And now, sir, what are your commands'?"

"I'll have sent for ye, Jack," begins Shipowner Younger, portentously lengthening the while his shaven upper-lip—"I'll have sent for ye, for three several matters: To pay ye a compliment or twa; to gi' ye a gude lecture; an' lastly to do a trifle of business wi' ye, by way of rounding off. For I hold," goes on Shipowner Younger, in an admonishing tone, "that conversations which don't carry a trifle of business are no mair than just the crackle of thorns under a pot. Ye'll ken I'm rich, Jack—ye'll ken I can clink my gold, an' count my gold, an' keep my gold wi' the warmest mon in Whitehaven?"

Young Jack Paul smiles, and nods his full agreement.

"But ye'll no ken," goes on Shipowner Younger, with proud humility, the pride being real and the humility imitated—"ye'll no ken, I believe, that I'm 'lected to the Parleyment in Lunnon, lad?" Shipowner Younger pauses to observe the effect of this announcement of his greatness. Being satisfied, he goes on. "It's a sacrifeece, no doot, but I s'all make it. The King has need of my counsel; an', God save him! he s'all have it. For I've always said, lad, that a mon's first debt is to the King. But it'll mean sore changes, Jack, sore changes will it mean; for I'm to sell up my ships to the last ship's gig of 'em, the better to leave me hand-free and head-free to serve the King."

Young Jack Paul is polite enough to arch his brows and draw a serious face. Shipowner Younger is pleased at this, and, with a deprecatory wave of his hand, as one who dismisses discussion of misfortunes which are beyond the help of words, proceeds:

"But enou' of idle clavers; I'll e'en get to what for I brought you here." Shipowner Younger leans far back in his big chair, and contemplates young Jack Paul with a twinkle. "Now, lad," he begins, "when from 'prentice ye are come to be first mate among my ships, I'm to tell ye that from Dick Bennison who signed ye, to Ed'ard Denbigh whose first officer ye now be, all the captains ye've sailed wi' declare ye a finished seaman. But"—here Shipowner Younger shakes his head as though administering reproof—"they add that ye be ower handy wi' your fists."

"Why, then," breaks in young Jack Paul, "how else am I to keep my watch in order! Besides, I hold it more humane to strike with your fist than with a belaying pin. The captains, I'll warrant, have told you I thrashed none but ship's bullies."

"They'll have told me nothing of the kind," returns Shipowner Younger. "They said naught of bullies. What they did observe was that ye just pounded the faces of the fo'c'sle hands in the strict line of duty. Why, they said the whole ship's crew loved ye like collie dogs! It seems ye've a knack of thrashing yourself into their hearts."

Young Jack Paul's eyes show pleasure and relief; he perceives he is not being scolded.

"And now," says Shipowner Younger, donning the alert manner of your true-born merchant approaching pounds, shillings and pence—"and now, having put the compliments and the lecture astern, we'll even get doon to business. As I was tellin', I'm about to retire from the ships. I'm rich enou'; and, being called to gi' counsel to the King, I want no exter-aneous interests to distract me. The fair truth is, I've sold all but the bark ye're now wi', the John O' Gaunt, ye'll ken; and that's to be sold to-day."

"You'll sell our John O' Gaunt, sir? Who is to own it?"

"Ed'ard Denbigh, your captain, is to own five-sixths of her, for which he'll pay five thousand pounds; being dog-cheap"—here a deep sigh—"as I'm a Christian! As for the remaining sixth, lad, why it's to be yours. Ye'll sail oot o' Whitehaven this v'yage in your own ship, partners wi' Ed'ard Denbigh."

"But, sir," protests young Jack Paul, his voice startled into a tremor, "with all thanks for your goodness, I've got no thousand pounds. You know the wages of a mate."

"Ay! I ken the wages of a mate weel enou'; I've been payin' 'em for thirty year come New Year's day. But ye'll no need money, Jack!"—the dry, harsh tones grow soft with kindliness—"ye'll no need money, mon, and there's the joke of it. For I'm to gi' ye your one-sixth of the John O' Gaunt, wi' never a shillin' from your fingers, and so make a man and a merchant of ye at a crack. Now, no words, lad! Ye've been faithful; and I've no' forgot that off Cape Clear one day ye saved me a ship. Ay! ye'll ken by now that Jamie Younger, for all he's 'lected to Parleyment to tell the King his mind, is no so giddy wi' his honors as to forget folk who serve him. No words, I tell ye! There ye be, sailor and shipowner baith, before ye're twenty-one. An' gude go wi' ye!"

The big-hearted Scotchman smothers the gratitude on the lips of young Jack Paul, and hands him out the door. As the latter goes down the stair, Shipowner Younger calls after him with a kind of anticipatory crow of exultation:

"And, lad! if ye get ever to Lunnon, come doon to Westminster, and see me just passin' the laws!"

The John O' Gaunt lies off the Guinea coast. The last one of its moaning, groaning, black cargo of slaves has come over the side from the shore boats, and been conveyed below. The John O' Gaunt has been chartered by a Bristol firm to carry three thousand slaves from the Guineas to Kingston; it will require ten voyages, and this is the beginning of the first.

The three hundred unhappy blacks who make the cargo are between decks. There they squat in four ranks, held by light wrist-chains to two great iron cables which are stretched forward and aft.

There are four squatting ranks of them; each rank sits face to face with its fellow rank across the detaining cable. Thus will they sit and suffer, cramped and choked and half-starved in that tropical hell between decks, through those two-score days and nights which lie between the John O' Gaunt and Kingston.

Captain Denbigh keeps the deck until the anchors are up. The wind is forward of the beam, and now, when its canvas is shaken out, the John O' Gaunt begins to move through the water on the starboard tack. The motion is slow and sulky, as though the ship were sick in its heart at the vile traffic it has come to, and must be goaded by stiffest gales before it consents to any show of speed. Captain Denbigh leaves the order, "West by north!" with second mate Boggs, who has the watch on deck; and, after glancing aloft at the sails and over the rail at the weather, waddles below to drink "Prosperous voyage!" with his first mate and fellow owner, young Jack Paul.

He finds that youthful mariner gloomy and sad.

The cabin where the two are berthed is roomy. At one end is a case of bottles—brandy and rum, the property of Captain Denbigh. At the other is a second lock-fast case, filled with books, the sailing companions of first mate Jack Paul. There are text-books—French, Spanish, Latin and Greek; for first mate Jack Paul is of a mind to learn languages during his watch below. There are books on navigation and astronomy, as well as volumes by De Foe and Richardson. Also, one sees the comedies of Congreve, and the poems of Alexander Pope. To these latter, first mate Jack Paul gives much attention; his inquiring nose is often between their covers. He studies English elegancies of speech and manner in Congreve, Pope and Richardson, while the crop-eared De Foe feeds his fancy for adventure.

As Captain Denbigh rolls into the cabin, first mate Jack Paul is not thinking on books. He has upon his mind the poor black wretches between decks, the muffled murmur of whose groans, together with the clanking of their wrist-chains, penetrates the bulkhead which forms the forward cabin wall. Captain Denbigh never heeds the silence and the sadness of his junior officer and partner, but marches, feet spread wide and sailorwise, to the locker which holds his bottles. Making careful selection, he brings out one of rum and another of sherry.

"You not likin' rum," explains Captain Denbigh, as he sets the sherry within reach of first mate Jack Paul.

First mate Jack Paul mechanically fills himself a moderate glass, while Captain Denbigh does himself more generous credit with a brimmer from the rum bottle.

"Here's to the good ship John O' Gaunt," cries Captain Denbigh, tossing the rum down his capacious throat. "May it live to carry niggers a hundred years!"

There is no response to this sentiment; but Captain Denbigh doesn't feel at all slighted, and sits down comfortably to the floor-fast table, the rum at his elbow. Being thus disposed, he glances at his moody companion.

There is much that is handsome in a rough, saltwater way about Captain Denbigh. He is short, stout, with a brown pillar of a throat, and shoulders as square as his yardarms. His thick hair is clubbed into a cue; there are gold rings in his ears, and his gray eyes laugh as he looks at you.

"An' now, mate Jack," says Captain Denbigh, cheerfully, "with our three hundred niggers stowed snug, an' we out'ard bound for Jamaica, let you an' me have a bit of talk. Not as cap 'in an' mate, mind you, but as owners. To begin with, then, you don't like the black trade?"

First mate Jack Paul looks up; the brown eyes show trouble and resolve.

"Captain," he says, "it goes against my soul!" Then, he continues apologetically: "Not that I say aught against slavery, which I've heard chaplains and parsons prove to be right and pious by Bible text. Ay! I've heard them when I've been to church ashore, with my brother William by the Rappahannock. My kinsman Jones owns slaves; and I can see, too, that they have safer, happier lives with him than could fall to their lot had they remained savages in the wild Guinea woods. But owning slaves by the Rappahannock, where you can give them kindness and make them happy, is one thing. This carrying the tortured creatures —chained, and mad with grief!—to Jamaica is another."

Captain Denbigh refreshes himself with more rum.

"It wards off the heat," he vouchsafes, in extenuation of his partiality for the rum. Having set himself right touching rum, he takes, up the main question: "What can we do?" he asks. "You know we're chartered for ten v'yages?"

"I'm no one to argue with my captain," responds first mate Jack Paul. "Still less do I talk of breaking charters. All I say is, it makes me heart-sore."

"Let me see!" responds Captain Denbigh, searching for an idea. "Your brother William tells me, the last time we takes in tobacco from the Jones plantation, that old William Jones is as fond o' you as o' him?"

"That is true. He wanted me to stay ashore with him and William, and give up the sea."

"An' why not, mate Jack?"

First mate Jack Paul shrugs his shoulders, which, despite his youth, are as broad and square as his captain's.

"Because I like the sea," says he; "and shall always like the sea."

Captain Denbigh takes more rum; after which he sits knitting his forehead into knots, in a very agony of cogitation. Finally he gives the table a great bang, at which the rum bottle jumps in alarm.

"I've hit it!" he cries. "I knowed I would if I'd only drink rum enough. I never has a bright idea yet, I don't get it from rum. Here, now, mate Jack; I'll just buy you out. You don't like the black trade, an' you'll like it less an' less. It's your readin' books does it; that, an not drinkin rum. Howsumever, I'll buy you out. Then you can take a merchant-ship; or—an' you may call me no seaman if that ain't what I'd do you sits down comfortable with your brother an' your old kinsman Jones by the Rappahannock, an plays gentleman ashore."

While Captain Denbigh talks, the trouble fades from the face of first mate Jack Paul.

"What's that?" he cries. "You'll buy me out?"

"Ay, lad! as sure as my name's Ed'ard Denbigh. That is, if so be you can sell, bein' under age. I allows you can, howsumever; for you're no one to go back on a bargain." Having thus adjusted to his liking the legal doubt suggested, Captain Denbigh turns to the question of price. "Master Younger puts your sixth at a thousand pounds. If so be you'll say the word, mate Jack, I'll give you a thousand pounds."

Countenance brightened with a vast relief, first mate Jack Paul stretches his hand across the table. Captain Denbigh, shifting his glass to the left hand, grasps it.

"Done!" says first mate Jack Paul.

"An' done to you, my hearty!" exclaims Captain Denbigh. "The money'll be yours, mate Jack, as soon as ever we sees Kingston light. An' now for another hooker of rum to bind the bargain."

CHAPTER III
THE YELLOW JACK

At Kingston, Captain Denbigh goes ashore with first mate Jack Paul, and pays over in Bank of England paper those one thousand pounds which represent that one-sixth interest in the John O'Gaunt. While the pair are upon this bit of maritime business, the three hundred mournful blacks are landed under the supervision of the second mate. Among the virtues which a cargo of slaves possesses over a shipment of cotton or sugar or rum, is the virtue of legs. This merit is made so much of by the energetic second officer of the John O'Gaunt, that, within half a day, the last of the three hundred blacks is landed on the Kingston quay. Received and receipted for by a bilious Spaniard with an umbrella hat, who is their consignee, the blacks are marched away to the stockade which will confine them while awaiting distribution among the plantations. Captain Denbigh puts to sea with the John O'Gaunt in ballast the same evening. A brisk seaman, and brisker man of business, is Captain Denbigh, and no one to spend money and time ashore, when he may be making the one and saving the other afloat.

First mate Jack Paul, his fortune of one thousand pounds safe in the strongboxes of the Kingston bank, sallies forth to look for a ship. He decides to go passenger, for the sake of seeing what it is like, and his first thought is to visit his brother William by the Rappahannock. This fraternal venture he forbears, when he discovers Kingston to be in the clutch of that saffron terror the yellow fever. Little is being locally said of the epidemic, for the town is fearful of frightening away its commerce. The Kingston heart, like most human hearts, thinks more of its own gold than of the lives of other men. Wherefore Kingston is sedulous to hide the plague in its midst, lest word go abroad on blue water and drive away the ships.

First mate Jack Paul becomes aware of Kingston for the death-trap it is before he is ashore two days. It is the suspicious multitude of funerals thronging the sun-baked streets, that gives him word. And yet the grewsome situation owns no peculiar threat for him, since he has sailed these blistering latitudes so often and so much that he may call himself immune. For him, the disastrous side is that, despite the Kingston efforts at concealment, a plague-whisper drifted out to sea, and as a cautious consequence the Kingston shipping has dwindled to be nothing. This scarcity of ships vastly interferes with that chance of a passage home.

"The first craft, outward bound for England, shall do," thinks first mate Jack Paul. "As to William, I'll defer my visit until I may go ashore to him without bringing the yellow jack upon half Virginia."

While waiting for that home-bound ship, first mate Jack Paul goes upon a pilgrimage of respect to the tomb of Admiral Benbow. That sea-wolf lies buried in the parish chapel-yard in King Street.

As first mate Jack Paul leaves the little burying-ground, he runs foul of a polite adventure which, in its final expression, will have effect upon his destiny. His aid is enlisted in favor of a lady in trouble.

The troubled lady, fat, florid and forty, is being conveyed along King Street in her ketureen, a sort of sedan chair on two wheels, drawn by a half-broken English horse. The horse, excited by a funeral procession of dancing, singing, shouting blacks, capsizes the ketureen, and the fat, florid one is decanted upon the curb at the feet of first mate Jack Paul. Alive to what is Christian in the way of duty, he raises the florid, fat decanted one, and congratulates her upon having suffered no harm.

The ketureen is restored to an even keel. The fat, florid one boards it, though not before she invites first mate Jack Paul to dinner. Being idle, lonesome, and hungry for English dishes, he accepts, and accompanies the fat, florid one in the dual guise of guest and bodyguard.

Sir Holman Hardy, husband to the fat, florid one, is as fatly florid as his spouse. Incidentally he is in command of what British soldiers are stationed at Kingston. The fat, florid one presents first mate Jack Paul to her Hector, tells the tale of the rescue, and thereupon the three go in to dinner. Later, first mate Jack Paul and his host smoke in the deep veranda, where, during the cool of the evening, Sir Holman drinks sangaree, and first mate Jack Paul drinks Madeira. Also Sir Holman inveighs against the Horse Guards for consigning him to such a pit of Tophet as is Kingston.

Between sangaree and maledictions levelled at the Horse Guards, Sir Holman gives first mate Jack Paul word of a brig, the King George's Packet, out of China for Kingston with tea, which he looks for every day. Discharging its tea, the King George's Packet will load with rum for Whitehaven; and Sir Holman declares that first mate Jack Paul shall sail therein, a passenger-guest, for home. Sir Holman is able to promise this, since the fat, florid rescued one is the child of Shipowner Donald of Donald, Currie & Beck, owners of the King George's Packet.

"Which makes me," expounds Sir Holman, his nose in the sangaree, "a kind of son-in-law to the brig itself."

He grumblingly intimates—he is far gone in sangaree at the time—that a fleet of just such sea-trinkets as the King George's Packet, so far as he has experimented with the marital condition, constitutes the one redeeming feature of wedlock.

"And so," concludes the excellent Sir Holman, "you're to go home with the rum, guest of the ship itself; and the thing I could weep over is that I cannot send my kit aboard and sail with you."

Two days go by, and the King George's Packet is sighted off Port Royal; twenty-four hours later its master, Captain Macadam——a Solway man——is drinking Sir Holman's sangaree. Making good his word, Sir Holman sends for first mate Jack Paul, and that business of going passenger to Whitehaven is adjusted.

"True!" observes Captain Macadam, when he understands—"true, the George isn't fitted up for passengers. But"—turning to first mate Jack Paul—"you'll no mind; bein' a seaman yours eh?"

"More than that, Captain," breaks in Sir Holman, "since the port is reeling full of yellow jack, some of your people might take it to sea with them. Should aught go wrong, now, why here is your passenger, a finished sailorman, to give you a lift."

Captain Macadam's face has been tanned like leather. None the less, as he hears the above the mahogany hue thereof lapses into a pasty, piecrust color. Plainly that word yellow jack fills his soul with fear. He mentions the wearisome fact to first mate Jack Paul, as he and that young gentleman, after their cigars and sangaree with Sir Holman, are making a midnight wake for the change house whereat they have bespoken beds.

"It's no kindly," complains Captain Macadam, "for Sir Holman to let me run my brig blindfold into sic a snare. But then he has a fourth share in the tea, and another in the rum; and so, for his profit like, he lets me tak' my chances. He'd stude better wi' God on high I'm thinkin', if he'd let his profit gone by, and just had a pilot boat standin' off and on at Port Royal, to gi' me the wink to go wide. I could ha' taken the tea to New York weel enou'. But bein' I'm here," concludes the disturbed Captain, appealing to first mate Jack Paul, "what would ye advise?"

"To get your tea ashore and your rum aboard as fast as you may."

"Ay! that'll about be the weesdom of it!"

Captain Macadam can talk of nothing but yellow jack all the way to the change house.

"It's the first time I was ever in these watters," he explains apologetically, "and now I can smell fever in the air! Ay! the hond o' death is on these islands! Be ye no afeard, mon?"

First mate Jack Paul says that he is not. Also he is a trifle irritated at the alarm of the timorous Captain Macadam.

"That'll just be your youth now!" observes the timorous one. "Ye're no old enou' to grasp the responsibeelities."

At four in the morning Captain Macadam comes into first mate Jack Paul's room at the change house. He is clad in his linen sleeping suit, and his teeth are chattering a little.

"It's the bein' ashore makes my teeth drum," he vouchsafes. "But what I wushed to ask ye, lad, is d'ye believe in fortunes? No? Weel, then, neither do I; only I remembered like that lang syne a wierd warlock sort o' body tells me in the port o' Leith, that I'm to meet my death in the West Injies. It's the first time, as I was tellin' ye, that ever I comes pokin' my snout amang these islands; and losh! I believe that warlock chiel was right. I've come for my death sure."

Captain Macadam promises his crew' double grog and double wages, and works night and day lightering his tea ashore, and getting his rum casks into the King George's Packet. Then he calls a pilot, and, with a four-knot breeze behind him, worms his way along the narrow, corkscrew channel, until he finds himself in open water.

Then the pilot goes over the side, and Captain Macadam takes the brig. He casts an anxious eye astern at Port Royal, four miles away.

"I'll no feel safe," says he, "while yon Satan's nest is under my quarter. And afterward I'll no feel safe neither. How many days, mon, is a victeem to stand by and look for symptoms?"

First mate Jack Paul, to whom the query is put, gives it as his opinion that, if they have yellow fever aboard, it will make its appearance within the week.

"Weel that's a mercy ony way!" says Captain Macadam with a sigh.

There are, besides first mate Jack Paul, and the Captain with his two officers, twelve seamen and the cook—seventeen souls in all—aboard the King George's Packet as, north by east, it crawls away from Port Royal. For four days the winds hold light but fair. Then come head winds, and the brig finds itself making long tacks to and fro in the Windward Passage, somewhere between Cape Mazie and the Mole St. Nicholas.

"D'ye see, mon!" cries Captain Macadam, whose fears have increased, not diminished, since he last saw the Jamaica lights. "The vera weather seeks to keep us in this trap! I'll no be feelin' ower weel neither, let me tell ye!"

First mate Jack Paul informs the alarmed Captain that to fear the fever is to invite it.

"I'm no afeard, mon," returns Captain Macadam, with a groan, "I'm just impressed."

The timidities of the Captain creep among the mates and crew; forward and aft the feeling is one of terror. The King George's Packet becomes a vessel of gloom. There are no songs, no whistling for a wind. Even the cook's fiddle is silent, and the galley grows as melancholy as the forecastle.

It is eight bells in the afternoon of the fourth day, when the man at the wheel calls to Captain Macadam. He tosses his thumb astern.

"Look there!" says he.

Captain Macadam peers over the rail, and counts eleven huge sharks. The monsters are following the brig. Also, they seem in an ugly mood, since ever and anon they dash at one another ferociously.

"It'll be a sign!" whispers Captain Macadam. Then he counts them. "There'll be 'leven o' them," says he; "and that means we're 'leven to die!" After this he dives below, and takes to the bottle.

Bleared of eye, shaken of hand, Captain Macadam on the fifth morning finds first mate Jack Paul on the after deck. The eleven sharks are still sculling sullenly along in the slow wake of the wind-bound brig.

"Be they there yet?" asks Captain Macadam, looking over the stern with a ghastly grin. Then answering his own query: "Ay! they'll be there—the 'leven of 'em!"

First mate Jack Paul, observing their daunting effect on the over-harrowed nerves of Captain Macadam, is for having up his pistols to take a shot at the sharks; but he is stayed by the other.

"They'll be sent," says Captain Macadam; "it'll no do to slay 'em, mon! But losh! ain't a sherk a fearfu' feesli?" Then, seeing his hand shake on the brig's rail: "It's the rum. And that's no gude omen, me takin' to the rum; for I'm not preeceesely what you'd ca' a drinkin' body."

Two hours later Captain Macadam issues from his cabin and seeks first mate Jack Paul, where the latter is sitting in the shade of the main sail.

"Mon, look at me!" he cries. "D'ye no see? I tell ye, Death has found me oot on the deep watters!"

The single glance assures first mate Jack Paul that Captain Macadam is right. His eyes are congested and ferrety; his face is flushed. Even while first mate Jack Paul looks, he sees the skin turn yellow as a lemon. He thumbs the sick man's wrist; the pulse is thumping like a trip-hammer. Also, the dry, fevered skin shows an abnormal temperature.

"Your tongue!" says first mate Jack Paul; for he has a working knowledge of yellow jack.

It is but piling evidence upon evidence; the tongue is the color of liver. Three hours later, the doomed man is delirious. Then the fever gives way to a chill; presently he goes raving his way into eternity, and the King George's Packet loses its Captain.

First mate Jack Paul sews the dead skipper in a hammock with his own fingers; since, mates, crew and cook, not another will bear a hand. When the hammock sewing is over, the cook aids in bringing the corpse on deck. As the body slips from the grating into the sea, a thirty-two pound shot at the heels, the cook laughs overboard at the sharks, still hanging, like hounds upon a scent, to the brig's wake.

"Ye'll have to dive for the skipper, lads!" sings out the cook.

Offended by this ribaldry, first mate Jack Paul is on the brink of striking the cook down with a belaying pin. For his own nerves are a-jangle, and that misplaced merriment rasps. It is the look in the man's face which stays his hand.

"Ye'll be right!" cries the cook, as though replying to something in the eye of first mate Jack Paul. "Don't I know it? It is I who'll follow the skipper! I'll just go sew my own hammock, and have it ready, shot and all."

As the cook starts for the galley, a maniac yell is heard from the forecastle. At that, he pauses, sloping his ear to listen.

"I'll have company," says he.

First the cook; then the mates; then seven of the crew. One after the other, they follow a thirty-two pound shot over the side; for after the Captain's death the sailors lose their horror of the plague-killed ones, and sew them up and slip them into the sea as readily as though they are bags of bran. The worst is that a fashion of dull panic takes them, and they refuse their duty. There is no one to command, they say; and, since there can be no commands, there can be no duty. With that they hang moodily about the capstan, or sulk in their bunks below.

First mate Jack Paul takes the wheel, rather than leave the King George's Packet to con itself across the ocean. As he is standing at the wheel trying to make a plan to save the brig and himself, he observes a sailor blundering aft. The man dives below, and the next moment, through the open skylights, first mate Jack Paul hears him rummaging the Captain's cabin. In a trice, he lashes the wheel, and slips below on the heels of the sailor. As he surmises, the man is at the rum. Without word spoken, he knocks the would-be rum guzzler over, and then kicks him up the companion way to the deck.

Pausing only to stick a couple of pistols in his belt, first mate Jack Paul follows that kicked seaman with a taste for rum. He walks first to the wheel. The wind is steady and light; for the moment the brig will mind itself. Through some impulse he glances over the stern; the sharks are gone. This gives him a thought; he will use the going of the sharks to coax the men.

The five are grouped about the capstan, the one who was struck is bleeding like tragedy. First mate Jack Paul makes them a little speech.

"There are no more to die," says he. "The called-for eleven are dead, and the sharks no longer follow us. That shows the ship free of menace; we're all to see England again. And now, mates"—there is that in the tone which makes the five look up—"I've a bit of news. From now, until its anchors are down in Whitehaven basin, I shall command this ship."

"You?" speaks up a big sailor. "You're no but a boy!"

"I'm man enough to sail the brig to England, and make you work like a dog, you swab!" The look in the eye of first mate Jack Paul, makes the capstan quintette uneasy. He goes on: "Come, my hearties, which shall it be? Sudden death? or you to do your duty by brig and owners? For, as sure as ever I saw the Solway, the first who doesn't jump to my order, I'll plant a brace of bullets in his belly!"

And so rebellion ceases; the five come off their gloomings and their grumblings, and spring to their work of sailing the brig. It is labor night and day, however, for all aboard; but the winds blow the fever away, the gales favor them, one and all they seem to have worn out the evil fortune which dogged them out of Kingston. The King George's Packet comes safe, at the last of it, into Whitehaven—first mate Jack Paul and his crew of five looking for the lack of sleep like dead folk walking the decks.

Donald, Currie & Beck pay a grateful salvage on brig and cargo to first mate Jack Paul and the five, for bringing home the brig. This puts six hundred pounds into the pockets of first mate Jack Paul, and one-fifth as much into the pockets of each of the five. Then Donald, Currie & Beck have first mate Jack Paul to dinner with the firm.

"We've got a ship for ye," says shipowner Donald, as the wine is being passed. "Ye're to be Captain."

"Captain!" repeats first mate Jack Paul. "A ship for me?"

"Who else, then!" returns shipowner Donald. "Ay! it's the Crantully Castle, four hundred tons, out o' Plymouth for Bombay. Ye're to be Captain; besides, ye're to have a tenth in the cargo. And now if that suits ye, gentlemen"—addressing shipowners Currie & Beck—"let the firm of Donald, Currie & Beck fill up the glasses to the Crantully Castle and its new Captain, Jack Paul."

CHAPTER IV
THE KILLING OF MUNGO

Captain Jack Paul and his Grantully Castle see friendly years together. They go to India, to Spain, to the West Indies, to the Mediterranean, to Africa. While Captain Jack Paul is busy with the Grantully Castle, piling up pounds and shillings and pence for owners Donald, Currie & Beck, he is also deep with the books, hammering at French, Spanish and German. Ashore, he makes his way into what best society he can find, being as eager to refine his manners as refine his mind, holding the one as much an education as is the other. Finally he is known in every ocean for the profundity of his learning, the polish of his deportment, the power of his fists, and the powder-like explosiveness of his temper.

It is a cloudy October afternoon when Captain Jack Paul works the Grantully Castle out of Plymouth, shakes free his canvas, and fills away on the starboard tack for Tobago. The crew is an evil lot, and a spirit of mutiny stirs in the ship. Captain Jack Paul, who holds that a good sailor is ever a good grumbler, can overlook a deal in favor of this aphorism; and does. On the sixth day out, however, when his first officer, Mr. Sands, staggers below with a sheath-knife through his shoulder, it makes a case to which no commander can afford to seem blind.

"It was Mungo!" explains the wounded Mr. Sands.

Captain Jack Paul goes on deck, and takes his stand by the main mast.

"Pipe all hands aft, Mr. Cooper," he says to the boatswain.

The crew straggle aft. They offer a circling score of brutal faces; in each the dominant expression is defiance.

"The man Mungo!" says Captain Jack Paul. "Where is he?"

At the word, a gigantic black slouches out from among his mates. Sloping shoulders, barrel body, long, swinging arms like a gorilla's, bandy legs, huge hands and feet, head the size and shape of a cocoanut, small, black serpent eyes, no soul unless a fiend's soul, Mungo is at once tyrant, pride and leader of the forecastle. Rumor declares that he has sailed pirate in his time, and should be sun-drying in chains on the gibbet at Corso Castle.

As he stands before Captain Jack Paul, Mungo's features are in a black snarl of fury. It is in his heart to do murderously more for his captain than he did for first officer Sands. He waits only the occasion before making a spring.

Captain Jack Paul looks him over with a grim stare as he slouches before him.

"Mr. Cooper," says Captain Jack Paul after a moment, during which he reads the black Mungo like a page of print, "fetch the irons!"

The boatswain is back on deck with a pair of steel wristlets in briefest space. He passes them to Captain Jack Paul. At this, Mungo glowers, while the mutinous faces in the background put on a dull sullenness. There are a brace of pistols in the belt of Captain Jack Paul, of which the sullen dull ones do not like the look. Mungo, a black berserk, cares little for the pistols, seeing he is in a white-hot rage, the hotter for being held in present check. Captain Jack Paul, on his part, is in no wise asleep; he notes the rolling, roving, bloodshot eye, like the eye of a wild beast at bay, and is prepared.

"Hold out your hands!" comes the curt command.

Plainly it is the signal for which Mungo waited. With a growling roar, bearlike in its guttural ferocity, he rushes upon Captain Jack Paul. The roaring rush is of the suddenest, but the latter is on the alert. Quick as is Mungo, Captain Jack Paul is quicker. Seizing a belaying-pin, he brings it crashing down on the skull of the roaring, charging black. The heavy, clublike pin is splintered; Mungo drops to the deck, a shivering heap. The great hands close and open; the muscles clutch and knot under the black skin; there is a choking gurgle. Then the mighty limbs relax; the face tarns from black to a sickly tallow. Mouth agape, eyes wide and staring, Mungo lies still.

Captain Jack Paul surveys the prostrate black. Then he tosses the irons to Boatswain Cooper.

"They will not be needed, Mr. Bo'sen," he says. "Pipe the crew for'ard!"

The keen whistle sings; the mutinous ones scuttle forward, like fowls that hear the high scream of some menacing hawk..

It is two bells in the evening; the port watch, in charge of the knife-wounded Mr. Sands, has the deck. The dead Mungo, tight-clouted in a hammock, lies stretched on a grating, ready for burial.

Captain Jack Paul comes up from his cabin. In his hand he carries a prayer-book. Also those two pistols are still in his belt.

"Turn out the watch below!" is the word.

The crew makes a silent half-circle about the dead Mungo. That mutinous sullenness, recently the defiant expression of their faces, is supplanted by a deprecatory look, composite of apology and fear. It is as though they would convince Captain Jack Paul of their tame and sheep-like frame of thought. The fate of Mungo has instructed them; for one and all they are of that criminal, coward brood, best convinced by a club and with whom death is the only conclusive argument. As they stand uncovered about the rigid one in the clouted hammock, they realize in full the villainy of mutiny, and abandon that ship-rebellion which has been forecastle talk and plan since ever the Plymouth lights went out astern.

Captain Jack Paul reads a prayer, and the dead Mungo is surrendered to the deep. As the body goes splashing into the sea, Captain Jack Paul turns on the subdued ones.

"Let me tell you this, my men!" says he. His tones have a cold, threatening ring, like the clink of iron on arctic ice. "The first of you who so much as lifts an eyebrow in refusal of an order shall go the same voyage as the black. And so I tell you!"

Captain Jack Paul brings the Grantully Castle into Tobago, crew as it might be a crew of lambs. Once his anchors are down, he signals for the port admiral. Within half an hour the gig of that dignitary is alongside.

The Honorable Simpson, Judge Surrogate of the Vice-Admiralty Court of Tobago, with the Honorable Young, Lieutenant-Governor of the colony, to give him countenance, opens court in the after cabins of the Grantully Castle. The crew are examined, man after man. They say little, lest they themselves be caught in some law net, and landed high and dry in the Tobago jail. First Officer Sands shows his wound and tells his story.

Throughout the inquiry Captain Jack Paul sits in silence, listening and looking on. He puts no questions to either mate or crew. When First Officer Sands is finished, the Honorable Simpson asks:

"Captain, in the killing of the black, Mungo, are you in conscience convinced that you used no more force than was necessary to preserve discipline in your ship?"

"May it please," returns Captain Jack Paul, who has not been at his books these years for nothing, and is fit to cope with a king's counsel —"may it please, I would say that it was necessary in the course of duty to strike the mutineer Mungo. This was on the high seas. Whenever it becomes necessary for a commanding officer to strike a seaman, it is necessary to strike with a weapon. Also, the necessity to strike carries with it the necessity to kill or disable the mutineer. I call your attention to the fact that I had loaded pistols in my belt, and could have shot the mutineer Mungo. I struck with a belaying-pin in preference, because I hoped that I might subdue him without killing him. The result proved otherwise. I trust your Honorable Court will take due account that, although armed with pistols throwing ounce balls, weapons surely fatal in my hands, I used a belaying-pin, which, though a dangerous, is not necessarily a fatal weapon."

Upon this statement, the Honorable Simpson and the Honorable Young confer. As the upcome of their conference, the Honorable Simpson announces judgment, exonerating Captain Jack Paul.

"The sailor Mungo, being at the time on the high seas, was in a state of mutiny." Thus runs the finding as set forth in the records of the Vice-Admiralty Court of Tobago. "The sailor Mungo was mutinous under circumstances which lodged plenary power in the hands of the master of the vessel. Therefore, the homicide was justifiable, because it had become the only means of maintaining the discipline required for the safety of the ship."

The court rises, and Captain Jack Paul bows the Honorable Simpson and the Honorable Young over the side. When they are clear, First Officer Sands addresses Captain Jack Paul.

"Are the crew to be set ashore, sir?" he asks.

"What! Mr. Sands, would you discharge the best crew we've ever had?" He continues as though replying to his first officer's look of astonishment. "I grant you they were a trifle uncurried at first. The error of their ways, however, broke upon them with all clearness in the going of Mungo. As matters now are, compared to the Grantully Castle, a dove-cote is a merest theatre of violence and murderous blood. No, Mr. Sands; we will keep our crew if you please. Should there be further mutiny, why then there shall be further belaying-pins, I promise you."

The Grantully Castle goes finally back to England, the most peaceful creature of oak and cordage that ever breasted the Atlantic. Cargo discharged, the ship is sent into winter overhaul.

"As for you, sir," remarks owner Donald, of Donald, Currie & Beck, shoving the wine across to Captain Jack Paul, "ye're just a maister mariner of gold! Ye'll no wait ashore for the Grantully Castle. We've been buildin' ye a new ship at our Portsmouth yards. She's off the ways a month, and s'uld be sparred and rigged and ready for the waves by now. We've called her The Two Friends."

CHAPTER V
THE SAILOR TURNS PLANTER

The wooded April banks of the Rappahannock are flourishing in the new green of an early Virginia spring. The bark Two Friends, Captain Jack Paul, out of Whitehaven by way of Lisbon, Madeira, and Kingston, comes picking her dull way up the river, and anchors midstream at the foot of the William Jones plantation. Almost coincident with the splash of the anchors, the Two Friends has her gig in the water, and the next moment Captain Jack Paul takes his place in the stern sheets.

"Let fall!" comes the sharp command, as he seizes the tiller-ropes.

The four sailors bend their strong backs, the four oars swing together like clockwork, and the gig heads for the plantation landing where a twenty-ton sloop, current-vexed, lies gnawing at her ropes.

At twenty-six, Captain Jack Paul is the very flower of a quarter-deck nobility. He has not the advantage of commanding height; but the lean, curved nose, clean jaw, firmly-lined month, steady stare of the brown eyes, coupled at the earliest smell of opposition with a frowning falcon trick of brow like a threat, are as a commission to him, signed and countersigned by nature, to be ever a leader of men. In figure he is five feet seven inches, and the scales telling his weight consent to one hundred and forty-five pounds. His hands and feet are as small as a woman's. By way of offset to this, his shoulders, broad and heavy, and his deep chest arched like the deck of a whale-back, speak of anything save the effeminate. In his movements there is a feline graceful accuracy> with over all a resolute atmosphere of enterprise. To his men, he is more than a captain; he is a god. Prudent at once and daring, he shines a master of seamanship, and never the sailor serves with him who would not name him a mariner without a flaw. He is born to inspire faith in men. This is as it should be, by his own abstract picture of a captain, which he will later furnish Doctor Franklin:

"Your captain," he will say, when thus informing that philosopher, "your captain, Doctor, should have the blind confidence of his sailors. It is his beginning, his foundation, wanting which he can be no true captain. To his men your captain must he prophet, priest and king. His authority when off-shore is necessarily absolute, and therefore the crew should be as one man impressed that the captain, like the sovereign, can do no wrong. If a captain fail in this, he cannot make up for it by severity, austerity or cruelty. Use force, apply restraint, punish as he may, he will always have a sullen crew and an unhappy ship."

The nose of the gig grates on the river's bank, and Captain Jack Paul leaps ashore. He is greeted by a tall, weather-beaten old man—grizzled and gray. The form of the latter is erect, with a kind of ramrod military stiffness. His dress is the rough garb of the Virginia overseer in all respects save headgear. Instead of the soft wool hat, common of his sort, the old man cocks over his watery left eye a Highland bonnet, and this, with its hawk's feather, fastened by a silver clasp, gives to his costume a crag and heather aspect altogether Scotch.

The gray old man, with a grinning background of negro slaves, waits for the landing of Captain Jack Paul. As the latter springs ashore, the old man throws up his hand in a military salute.

"And how do we find Duncan Macbean!" cries Captain Jack Paul. "How also is my brother! I trust you have still a bale or two of winter-cured tobacco left that we may add to our cargo!"

"As for the tobacco, Captain Paul," returns old Duncan Macbean, "ye're a day or so behind the fair, since the maist of it sailed Englandward a month back, in the brig Flora Belle. As for your brother William of whom ye ask, now I s'uld say ye were in gude time just to hear his dying words."

"What's that, Duncan Macbean!" exclaims Captain Jack Paul. "William dying!"

"Ay, dying! He lies nearer death than he's been any time since he and I marched with General Braddock and Colonel Washington, against the red salvages of the Ohio. But you s'uld come and see him at once, you his born brother, and no stand talking here."

"It's lung fever, Jack," whispers the sick man, as Captain Jack Paul draws a chair to the side of the bed. "It's deadly, too; I can feel it. I'll not get up again."

"Come, come, brother," retorts Captain Jack Paul cheerfully, "you're no old man to talk of death—you, with your fewer than fifty years. I'll see you up and on your pins again before I leave."

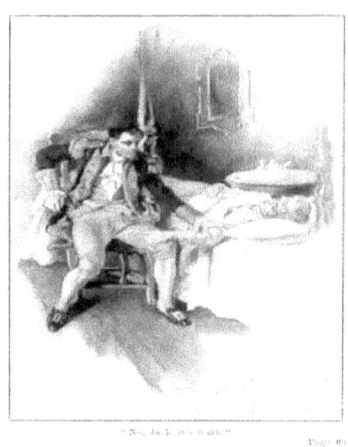

"No, Jack, it's death."

"No, Jack, it's death. And you've come in good time, too, since there's much to talk between us. You know how our cousin left me his heir, if I would take his name of Jones?"

"Assuredly I know."

"And so," continues the dying man, "my name since his passing away has been William Paul Jones. Now when it is my turn to go, I must tell you that, by a clause of the old man's will, he writes you in after me as legatee. I'm to die, Jack; and you're to have the plantation. Only you must clap 'Jones' to your name, and be not John Paul, but John Paul Jones, as you take over the estate."

"What's this? I'm to heir the plantation after you?"

"So declares the will. On condition, however, that you also take the name of Jones. That should not be hard; 'Jones' is one of our family names, and he that leaves you the land was our kinsman."

"Why, then," cries Captain Jack Paul, "I wasn't hesitating for that. Paul is a good name, but so also is Jones. Only, I tell you, brother, I hate to make my fortune by your death."

"That's no common-sense, Jack. I die the easier knowing my going makes way for your good luck. And the plantation's a gem, Jack; never a cold or sour acre in the whole three thousand, but all of it warm, sweet land. There're two thousand acres of woods; and I'd leave that stand." The dying man, being Scotch, would give advice on his deathbed. "The thousand acres now under plow are enough." Then, after a pause: "Ye'll be content ashore? You're young yet; you're not so wedded to the sea, I think, but you'll turn planter with good grace?"

"No fear, William. I've had good fortune by the sea; but then I've met ill fortune also. By and large, I shall be very well content to turn planter."

"It's gainful, Jack, being a planter is. Only keep Duncan Macbean by you to manage, and he'll turn you in one thousand golden guineas profit every Christmas day, and you never to lift hand or give thought to the winning of them."

"Is the plantation as gainful as that? Now I have but three thousand guineas to call mine, after sailing these years."

"Ay! it's gainful, Jack. If you will work, too, there's that to keep you busy. There's the grist mill, the thirty slaves, the forty horses, besides the cows and swine and sheep to look after; as well as the negro quarters, the tobacco houses, the stables, and the great mansion itself to keep up. They'll all serve to fill in the time busily, if you should like it that way. Only Jack, with the last of it, always leave everything to Duncan Macbean. A rare and wary man is old Duncan, and saving of money down to farthings."

"Whose sloop is that at the landing!" asks Captain Jack Paul, willing to shift the subject.

"Oh, yon sloop! She goes with the plantation; she'll be yours anon, brother. And there you are: When the sea calls to you, Jack, as she will call, you take the sloop. Cato and Scipio are good sailors, well trained to the coast clear away to Charleston."

And so William Paul Jones dies, and John Paul takes his place on the plantation. His name is no longer John Paul, but John Paul Jones; and, as his dying brother counselled, he keeps old Duncan Macbean to be the manager.

When his brother is dead, Captain Jack Paul joins his mate, Laurence Edgar, on the deck of the Two Friends, swinging tide and tide on her anchors.

"Mate Edgar," says Captain Jack Paul, "it is the last time I shall plank this quarterdeck as captain. I'm to stay; and you're to take the ship home to Whitehaven. And now, since you're the captain, and I'm no more than a guest, suppose you order your cabin boy to get us a bottle of the right Madeira, and we'll drink fortune to the bark and her new master."

CHAPTER VI
THE FIRST BLOW IN VIRGINIA

It is a soundless, soft December evening. The quietly falling flakes are cloaking in thin white the streets and roofs of Norfolk. Off shore, a cable's length, an English sloop of war, eighteen guns, lies tugging at her anchors. In shore from the sloop of war rides the peaceful twenty-ton sloop of Planter Paul Jones. The sailor-planter, loitering homeward from a cruise to Charleston and the coast towns of the Carolinas, is calling on friends in Norfolk. Both the war sloop and the peace sloop seem almost deserted in the falling snow. Aside from the harbor light burning high in the rigging, and an anchor watch of two sailors muffled to the ears, the decks of neither craft show signs of life.

Norfolk's public hall is candle-lighted to a pitch of unusual brilliancy; the waxed floors are thronged with the beauty and gentility of the Old Dominion, as the same find Norfolk expression. It is indeed a mighty social occasion; for the local élite have seized upon the officers of the sloop of war, and are giving a ball in their honor. The honored ones attend to a man—which accounts for the deserted look of their sloop—and their gold lace blazes bravely by the light of the candles, and with tremendous gala effect.

Planter Paul Jones is also among the guests. Since he is in town, his coming to the ball becomes the thing most natural. Already he is regarded as the Admirable Crichton, of tide-water Virginia, and the function wanting his presence would go down to history as incomplete.

Paul Jones, planter for two years, has made himself a foremost figure in Virginia. Twenty-eight, cultured, travelled, gallant, brilliant, and a bachelor, he is welcome in every drawing-room. Besides, is there not the Jones plantation, with its mile of river front, its noble mansion house, its tobacco teeming acres, its well-trained slaves, and all turning in those yearly one thousand yellow guineas under the heedful managing thumb of canny Duncan Macbean? Planter Paul Jones is a prince for hospitality, too; and the high colonial dames, taking pity on his wifeless state, preside at his table, or chaperone the water parties which he gives on his great sloop. Also—still considering his wifelessness—they seek to marry him to one of their colonial daughters.

In this latter dulcet intrigue, the high colonial dames fail wholly. The young planter-sailor is not a marrying man. There is in truth a blushing story which lasts throughout a fortnight in which he is quoted as about to yield.

Rumor gives it confidently forth that the Jones mansion will have a mistress, and its master carry altar-ward Betty Parke, the pretty niece of Madam Martha Washington. But pretty Betty Parke, in the very face of this roseate rumor, becomes Mrs. Tyler, and it will be one of her descendants who, seventy-five years later, is chosen President—a poor President, but still a President. Planter Paul Jones rides to the wedding of pretty Betty Parke, and gives it his serene and satisfied countenance. From which sign it is supposed that Dame Rumor mounts by the wrong stirrup when she goes linking the name of pretty Betty Parke with that of Planter Paul Jones; and no love-letter scrap, nor private journal note, will ever rise from the grave to disparage the assumption.

That Planter Paul Jones has thus lived for two years, and moved and had his social being among the most beautiful of women, and escaped hand free and heart free to tell the tale, is strange to the brink of marvellous. It is the more strange since no one could be more than he the knight of dames. And he can charm, too—as witness a letter which two years farther on the unimpressionable Doctor Franklin will write to Madam d'Haudetot:

"No matter, my dear madam," the cool philosopher will say, "what the faults of Paul Jones may be, I must warn your ladyship that when face to face with him neither man nor, so far as I learn, woman, can for a moment resist the strange magnetism of his presence, the indescribable charm of his manner; a commingling of the most compliant deference with the most perfect self-esteem that I have ever seen in a man; and above all the sweetness of his voice and the purity of his language."

Paul Jones is not alone the darling of colonial drawing-rooms, he is also the admiration of the men. This is his description as given by one who knew him afloat and ashore:

"Though of slender build, his neck, arms and shoulders were those of a heavy, powerful man. The strength of his arms and shoulders could hardly be believed. And he had equal use of both hands, even to writing with the left as well as with the right. He was a past master of the art of boxing. To this he added a quickness of motion that cannot be described. When roused he could strike more blows and cause more havoc in a second than any other could strike or cause in a minute. Even when calm and unruffled his gait and all his bodily motions were those of the panther—noiseless, sleek, the perfection of grace."

The above, by way of portrait: When one adds to it that Planter Paul Jones rides like a Prince Rupert, fences like a Crillon, gives blows with his fist that would stagger Jack Slack, and is death itself with either gun or pistol, it will be seen how he owns every quality that should pedestal him as a paragon in the best circles of his day.

It is towards the hour of midnight when Planter Paul Jones, attired like a Brummel, stands in quiet converse with his friend Mr. Hurst. Their talk runs on the state of sentiment in the colonies, and the chance of trouble with the motherland.

"Hostilities are certain, my dear Hurst," says Planter Paul Jones. "I hear it from Colonel Washington, Mr. Jefferson and Mr. Henry. They make no secret of it in Williamsburg about the House of Burgesses."

"But the other colonies'?"

"Mr. Morris of Philadelphia, as well as Mr. Pynckney of Charleston, agrees with the gentlemen I've quoted. They say, sir, there will soon be an outbreak in Boston."

"In Boston!" repeats Mr. Hurst doubtfully.

"Have the Massachusetts men the courage, think you?"

"Courage, ay! and the strength, my friend! Both Colonel Washington and Mr. Jefferson assured me that, although slow to anger, they are true sons of Cromwell's Ironsides.

"And what shall be our attitude?"

"We must sustain them at all hazards, sir—sustain them to the death!"

It is now that a knot of English officers drift up—a little flushed of wine, are these guests of honor. They, too, have been talking, albeit thickly, of a possible future full of trouble for the colonies.

"I was observing," says Lieutenant Parker, addressing Planter Paul Jones and Mr. Hurst, "that the insolence of the Americans, which is more or less in exhibition all the way from Boston to Savannah, will never get beyond words. There will be no blows struck."

"And why are you so confident?" asks Planter Paul Jones, eye agate, voice purringly soft. "Now I should say that, given provocation, the colonies would strike a blow, and a heavy one."

"When do you sail?" interrupts Mr. Hurst, speaking to Lieutenant Parker. Mr. Hurst would shift conversation to less perilous ground. As a mover of the ball, he is in sort host to the officers, as well as to Planter Paul Jones, and for the white credit of the town desires a peaceful evening. "I hear," he concludes, "that your sloop is for a cruise off the French coast."

"She and the fleet she belongs to," responds Lieutenant Parker, utterance somewhat blurred, "will remain on this station while a word of rebel talk continues."

"Now, instead of keeping you here," breaks in Planter Paul Jones, vivaciously, "to hector peaceful colonies, if I were your king I should send you to wrest Cape Good Hope from the Dutch."

"Cape Good Hope from the Dutch?"

"Or the Isles of France and Bourbon from the French—lying, as they do, like lions in the pathway to our Indian possessions. If I were your king, I say, those would be the tasks I'd set you."

"And why do you say 'your king?' Is he not also your king?"

"Why, sir, I might be pleasantly willing," observes Planter Paul Jones airily, "to give you my share in King George. In any event, I do not propose that you shall examine into my allegiance. And I say again that, if I were your king, sir, I'd find you better English work to do than an irritating and foolish patrol of these coasts."

"You spoke of the Americans striking a blow," says Lieutenant Parker, who is gifted of that pertinacity of memory common to half-drunken men; "you spoke but a moment back of the Americans striking a blow, and a heavy one."

"Ay, sir! a blow—given provocation."

Lieutenant Parker wags his head with an air of sagacity both bibulous and supercilious. He smiles victoriously, as a fortunate comparison bobs up to his mind.

"A blow!" he murmurs. Then, fixing Planter Paul Jones with an eye of bleary scorn: "The Americans would be quickly lashed into their kennels again. The more easily, if the courage of the American men, as I think's the case, is no more firmly founded than the chastity of the American women."

Planter Paul Jones deals Lieutenant Parker a blow with his clenched fist, the like of which was never before seen even in the violent port of Norfolk. Lieutenant Parker's nose is crushed flat with his face; he falls like some pole-axed ox. His fellow-officers lift him to his feet, bleeding, stunned beyond words.

"You shall hear from us!" is the fierce cry from his comrades, as they hurry the stricken Parker from the ballroom.

"I shall be pleased to hear from any or all of you," replies Planter Paul Jones; "or from what other dogs in king's coats shall question the honor of American women." Then, turning to Mr. Hurst: "You, sir, shall act for me! Accept every challenge they send! Make it pistols, ten paces, with Craney Island for the place; and fix the time to suit their English convenience."

CHAPTER VII
THE BLAST OF WAR

Norfolk is never more at peace than on the day succeeding the ball. There is no challenge, no duel. Planter Paul Jones waits to hear from Lieutenant Parker; at first hopefully; in the end, when nothing comes, with doubtful brow of grief. Is it that Lieutenant Parker will not fight? Planter Paul Jones hears the suggestion from his friend Mr. Hurst with polite scorn. Such heresy is beyond reach.

"He must fight," urges Planter Paul Jones, desperately keeping alive the fires of his hope. "He will fight, if for no other reason, then because it is his trade. Lieutenant Parker is pugnacious by profession; that of itself will make him toe the peg."

Planter Paul Jones is wrong. Lieutenant Parker never shows his beaten face on American soil again. Nor does any bellicose gentleman appear for Lieutenant Parker, or propose to take his place.

This last omission gives Planter Paul Jones as sharp a pang as though he has been slighted by some dearest friend. Having on his own part a native lust for battle, it bewilders him when so excellent a foundation for a duel falls into neglect, and no architect of combat steps forward to build thereon.

"It is not to be understood!" observes Planter Paul Jones dejectedly, after the sloop of war, with Lieutenant Parker and those others of that gold-lace coterie, has sailed away, "it's not to be understood! Surely, there must have been one gentleman among them who, free to do so, would have called me to account." Then, with solemn sadness: "I am convinced that their admiral interfered."

Who shall say? The admiral is the paternal uncle of Lieutenant Parker of the crushed and broken nose.

The story will go later to England to the explanatory effect that no fellow-officer would act for Lieutenant Parker. However, in doubt of this, that last named imprudent person—wearing the marks of Planter Paul Jones' rebuke for many a day—is not dismissed the king's service. He will be in the fight off Fort Moultrie, where—unlike Sergeant Jasper of the Americans—he in no wise is to distinguish himself.

Planter Paul Jones, when every final chance of the trouble for which he longs has departed with the departure of the war sloop, sorrowfully steers the peace sloop back to his plantation by the Rappahannock; and thereafter he does his best to forget an incident that—because of the mysterious tameness of the English, under conditions which should have brought them ferociously to the field—gives him an aching sense of pain. He says to Mr. Hurst, when about to spread his small canvas and sail away for home, "It is one of those experiences, sir, that shake a man's faith in his kind."

The colonial dames get hold of the tale, and

Planter Paul Jones becomes all the more the petted darling of the drawing-rooms. This of itself is a destiny most friendly to his taste; for our Virginia Bayard lives not without his tender vanities. Bright eyes are more beautiful than stars; and he can sigh, or whisper a sonnet, or softly press a little hand. Also, having in his composition an ardent dash of the peacock, he is capable, with fair ladies looking on, of a decorous, albeit a resplendent strut.

Four months, dating from the disaster to Lieutenant Parker's nose, have squeezed through the gates of a narrow present, and merged with those other countless months which together make the past. It is a muggy April morning, and New York City, panting with its metropolitan population of forty thousand, is soaked to the bone. Little squalls of rain follow each other in gusty procession. Between the squalls the sun shines forth, and sets the world a-steam. After each of these intermittent bursts of glory, the sun is again blotted ont by a black flurry of clouds, and another shower sets in.

It is in William Street that the reader comes across the lithe figure of Planter Paul Jones. That restless tobacco grower, with his two aquatic slaves, Scipio and Cato, in the little sloop, has been knocking about the eastern shore for ducks. A sudden change of plan now brings him to New York, with a final purpose of extending his voyage as far as Boston. Planter Paul Jones is in a mood to know the Yankees better, and come by some guess of his own as to how soon our Puritan bulldogs may be expected to fly at the English throat.

As he goes briskly northward along William Street, even through his landsman's garb there shows much that is marine. Also, he evinces a sailor's contempt for the dripping weather, plowing ahead through shine and through shower as though in the catalogue of the disagreeable there is no such word as a wetting.

At the corner of John Street, Planter Paul Jones comes upon a lean, prim personage. By his severe air the latter gentleman is evidently an individual of consequence. The severe gentleman, with a prudent care for his coat in direct contrast to the weather-carelessness of the other, has taken refuge in the safe harborage of a doorway. From the dry vantage thereof he cranes his neck in a tentative way, the better to survey the heavens. Plainly he desires a guarantee, in favor of some partial space of sunshine, before he again ventures abroad.

As Planter Paul Jones comes up, both he and the severe gentleman gaze at each other for one moment. Then their hands are caught in a warm exchange of greetings:

"Mr. Livingston, by my word!" cries Planter Paul Jones, shaking the severe gentleman's hand.

"Paul Jones!" exclaims the severe gentleman, returning the handshake, but with due regard to the pompous.

"Now this is what I term fortunate!" says Planter Paul Jones, releasing the other's fingers. "I was on my way to your house to ask for letters of introduction to Mr. Hancock and others in Boston."

"Boston! Surely you have heard the news?"

"News? I've heard nothing. For six weeks I've been anywhere between Barnegat and the inner Chesapeake in my sloop. I tied up at the foot of Whitehall Street within the hour, and you're the first I've spoken with since I stepped ashore. What is this news that makes you stare at the name of Boston?"

"And you've not heard!" repeats Mr. Livingston. Then, with a look at once somber and solemn: "Black news! Black news, indeed! I'm on my way to Hanover Square to have it set in types, and scattered up and down the town. Come; you shall go with me. I'll talk as we walk along."

Mr. Livingston takes Planter Paul Jones by the arm.

"Black news!" he resumes. "The Massachusetts men have attacked the British at Lexington and Concord; my despatches, while necessarily meager, declare that the British were disgracefully beaten, and lost, killed and wounded, several hundred soldiers."

"And you call that black news?" interjects Planter Paul Jones, his eye finely aflame. "To my mind now it is as good news as ever I hope to hear."

"How can you say so! It fills me with measureless gloom. I cannot but look ahead and wonder where it will end. And yet we should hope for the best." The speaker heaves a weary sigh. "Possibly the mother country may learn from this experience how bitterly in earnest Americans are, and be thereby led to mitigate the harshness of her attitude toward us."

Planter Paul Jones looks his emphatic disbelief.

"There will be no softening of England's attitude. Believe me, sir, I'm not so long out of London, but what I'm clear as to the plans and purposes of

King George and his ministers. The Tories have deliberately forced the present situation."

"Forced the situation! You amaze me!"

"Sir, my name is not Paul Jones, if it be not the deliberate design of King George and his advisers to bring about a clash between England and these colonies."

"And to what end, pray?"

"To give them an excuse for imposing martial law upon us. They will pour a cataract of redcoats upon our shores. Musket in fist, cannon to back them, they will disperse our legislatures, take away our charters of self-government. That blood at Concord and Lexington gives them the pretext for which they schemed. They can now call us 'rebels;' and, calling us 'rebels,' they will try to reduce us—for all our white skins and freeborn blood—to the slavish status of Hindostan."

Mr. Livingston stares, while this long speech is reeled off.

"Do you mean to say," he asks at last, "that we are the victims of a Tory plot? Am I to understand that Concord and Lexington were aimed at by the king?"

"Precisely so; and for one I'm glad the issue's made. We have now but the one alternative. We may choose between abject slavery and war to the hilts."

Mr. Livingston's severely pompons face, as the iron truth begins to overcome him, assumes an expression at once noble and high.

"Why, then!" says he, "if such be the Tory design, war we shall have." Then, following a pause: "And what is to be your course in case of war?"

"I shall take my part in it, never fear! This very day I shall write to friends who will have seats in the Congress that meets next month in Philadelphia, and ask them to wear my name in their minds. I am theirs so soon as ever they have a plank afloat to put me on."

The pair, earnestly talking, reach Hanover Square, and pause in front of "The Bible and Crown."

"Here we are," says Mr. Livingston. "Now if you'll but wait until I give orders to Master Rivington, as to how he shall print and circulate my despatches, I'll have you up to the house, where we can further consider this business over a bottle of wine."

"I beg that you will excuse me," returns Planter Paul Jones. He has been making plans of his own while they talked. "I trust you will pardon me; but

I shall have no more than time to write and post my letters, and get away on the ebb tide. Three days from now I must be at my plantation by the Rappahannock, putting all in order for the storm."

"Remember!" cries Mr. Livingston, as he and Planter Paul Jones shake hands at parting, "my brother Philip will be in the coming Congress. You have but to go to him, he is as much your friend as is either Mr. Washington or Mr. Jefferson. I shall speak to Philip of you before the day is out."

"Say to your brother," returns Planter Paul Jones, "that I shall come to him among the first."

The winds generously flatter the little sloop on her return voyage. She came north slowly, reluctantly; now, with the wind aft and all but blowing a gale, she flies southward like a bird. As Planter Paul Jones boasted, within the three days after seeing the last of Sandy Hook, he steps ashore on his own domain by the Rappahannock.

Cato and Scipio grin in exultation. In a pardonable anxiety to open the eyes of plodding fellow-slaves of the tobacco fields, they mendaciously shorten the sailing time out of New York by forty-eight hours, and declare that Planter Paul Jones brought the sloop home in a single day.

"Potch um home, Marse Paul does, faster than a wil' duck could trabble!" is their story. Thereupon, the innocent tobacco blacks marvel, openmouthed, at the far-travelled Cato, and Scipio of the many experiences.

Planter Paul Jones, on whom a war-fever is growing, plunges into immediate conference with Duncan Macbean.

"How much free money can we make?" he asks.

The old Highlander scratches his grizzled locks.

Then he thoughtfully considers the inside of his Glengarry bonnet, which he takes from his head for that purpose. One would think, from his long study of it, that he keeps his accounts in its linings. The inspection being over, he puts it back on his head.

"Now there s'uld be the matter of three thousand guineas in gold in Williamsburg," returns old Duncan Macbean; "besides a hunner or so siller in the house. I can gi' ye three thousand guineas, and never miss the feel o' them, gin that'll be enou'."

"Three thousand guineas! What time I shall be in Philadelphia it should keep a king! Have it set to my credit, Duncan, in Mr. Ross' bank in Chestnut Street in that town. I shall go there as soon as Congress convenes."

"And will ye no be back home agen?" asks Duncan, his bronzed cheek a trifle white.

"If there's war—and, take it from me, there will be—I shall not return. I hope to sail in the first warship that flies the colors of the Colonies."

Then, grasping old Duncan's hand in a grip of steel: "You stay here and run the plantation, old friend! Wherever I am, I shall know that all is right ashore while you are here. For I can trust you."

"Ay! ye can trust me; no fear o' that!" and the water stands in the old eyes.

CHAPTER VIII
THE PLANTER TURNS LIEUTENANT

It was Mr. Adams who opposed you. The best place I could make was that of lieutenant. Mr. Adams wouldn't hear of you as a captain; and since, with General Washington, Virginia and the Southern Colonies have been given control of the Army, his claim of the Navy for Massachusetts and the Northern Colonies finds general consent. Commodore Hopkins and four of the five captains, beginning with Mr. Adams' protégé Dudley Saltonstall, go to New England. The most that I could make Mr. Adams agree to, was that you should be set at the head of the list of lieutenants."

"I am sorry, sir, that Mr. Adams holds a poor opinion of me." This with a sigh. "It was my dream to be a captain, and have a ship of my own. However, I am here to serve the cause, rather than promote the personal fortunes of Paul Jones. Let the list go as it is; the future doubtless will bring all things straight. I am free to say, however, that from the selections made by Mr. Adams, as you repeat them, I think he has provided for more courts-martial than victories." The two gentlemen in talk are Mr. Hewes, member of the Colonial Congress from North Carolina, and Planter Paul Jones. Mr. Hewes is old and worn and sick, and only his granite resolution keeps him at the seat of government.

"Mr. Hancock," continues Mr. Hewes, "is also from Massachusetts, and as chairman of our committee he gave Mr. Adams what aid he could. There's one honor you may have, however; I arranged for that. The issuance of the commissions is with Mr. Hancock, and if you'll accompany me to the Hall you will be given yours at once. That will make you the first, if not the highest, naval officer of the Colonies to be commissioned."

"On what ship am I to serve?"

"The Alfred, Captain Saltonstall."

Raw and bleak sweep the December winds through the bare streets, as the two go on their way to the Hall, where Congress holds its sittings. Fortunately, as Lieutenant Paul Jones phrases it, the wind is "aft," and so Mr. Hewes, despite his weakness, makes better weather of it than one would look for.

"I'll have a carriage home," says he, panting a little, as the stiff breeze steals his breath away.

"I can't," breaks forth Lieutenant Paul Jones, after an interval of silence— "I can't for the life of me make out how I incurred the enmity of Mr. Adams. I've never set foot in Boston, never clapped my eyes on him before I came to this city last July."

Mr. Hewes smiles. "You sacrificed interest to epigram," says he. Lieutenant Paul Jones glares in wonder. "Let me explain," goes on Mr. Hewes, answering the look. "Do you recall meeting Mr. Adams at Colonel Carroll's house out near Schuylkill Falls?"

"That was last October."

"Precisely! Mr. Adams' memory is quite equal to last October. The more, if the event remembered were a dig to his vanity."

"A dig to his vanity!" repeats Lieutenant Paul Jones in astonishment. "I cannot now recall that I so much as spoke a word to the old polar bear."

"It wasn't a word spoken to him, but one spoken of him. This is it: Mr. Adams told an anecdote in French to little Betty Faulkner. Later you must needs be witty, and whisper to Miss Betty a satirical word anent Mr. Adams' French."

"Why, then," interjects Lieutenant Paul Jones, with a whimsical grin, "I'll tell you what I said. 'It is fortunate,' I observed to Miss Betty, 'that Mr. Adams' sentiments are not so English as is his French. If they were, he would far and away be the greatest Tory in the world.'"

"Just so!" chuckles Mr. Hewes. "And, doubtless, all very true. None the less, my young friend, your brightness cost you a captaincy. The mot was too good to keep, and little Betty started it on a journey that landed it, at a fourth telling, slap in the outraged ear of Mr. Adams himself. Make you a captain? He would as soon think of making you rich."

The pair trudged on in silence, Mr. Hewes turning about in his mind sundry matters of colonial policy, while Lieutenant Paul Jones solaces himself by recalling how it is the even year to a day since that Norfolk ball, when he smote upon the scandalous nose of Lieutenant Parker.

"Now that I'm a lieutenant like himself," runs the warlike cogitations of Lieutenant Paul Jones, "I'd prodigiously enjoy meeting the scoundrel afloat. I might teach his dullness a better opinion of us."

Lieutenant Paul Jones for months has been hard at work; one day in conference with the Marine Committee, leading them by the light of his ship-knowledge; the next busy with adz and oakum and calking iron, repairing and renewing the tottering hulks which the agents of the colonies have collected as the nucleus of the baby navy. Over this very ship the

Alfred, on which he is to sail lieutenant, he has toiled as though it were intended as a present for his bride. He confidently counted on being made its captain; now to sail as a subordinate, when he looked to have command, is a bitter disappointment. Sail he will, however, and that without murmur; for he is too much the patriot to hang back, too strong a heart to sulk. Besides, he has the optimism of the born war dog.

"Given open war," thinks he, "what more should one ask than a cutlass, and the chance to use it? Once we're aboard an enemy, it shall go hard, but I carve a captaincy out of the situation."

Congress is not in session upon this particular day, and Mr. Hewes leads Lieutenant Paul Jones straight to Chairman Hancock of the Marine Committee. That eminent patriot is in his committee room. He is big, florid, proud, and, like all the Massachusetts men since Concord and Lexington, a bit puffed up. No presentation is needed; Mr. Hancock and Lieutenant Paul Jones have been acquainted for months. The big merchant-statesman beams pleasantly on the new lieutenant. Then he draws Mr. Hewes into a far window.

"I can't see what's got into Adams," says Mr. Hancock, lowering his voice to a whisper. "He burst in here a moment ago, and declared that he meant to move, at the next session, a reconsideration of the appointment of our young friend."

"And now where pinches the shoe?"

"He says that Paul Jones isn't two years out of England; that his sympathies must needs lean toward King George."

"It will be news if the patriotism of Mr. Adams himself stands as near the perpendicular as does that of Paul Jones!"

"And next he urges that our friend is a man of no family."

"Now, did one ever hear such aristocratic bosh! The more, since our cause is the cause of human rights, and our shout 'Democracy!' I shall take occasion, when next I have the honor to meet Mr. Adams"—here the eyes of the old North Carolinian begin to sparkle—"to mention this subject of families, and remind him that it might worry the Herald's College excessively, if that seminary of pedigrees were called upon to back-track his own."

"No, no, my dear sir!" and the merchant-statesman, full of lofty mollifications, makes a soothing gesture with his hands. "For all our sakes, say nothing to Mr. Adams! You recall what Doctor Franklin remarked of him: 'He is always honest, sometimes great, but often mad.' Let us suppose him merely mad; and so forgive him. We may do it the more easily, since I told him that, even if his objections were valid, he was miles too late, the question of that lieutenancy having been already passed upon and settled. Let us forget Adams, and give Paul Jones his commission."

As Lieutenant Paul Jones receives his commission from Mr. Hancock, the latter remarks with a smile:

"You have the first commission issued, Lieutenant Jones. If the simile were permissible concerning anything that refers to the sea, I should say now that, in making you a lieutenant, we lay the corner stone of the American Navy."

"In making you a lieutenant we lay the cornerstone of the American Navy."

Lieutenant Paul Jones bows his thanks, but speaks never a word. This silence arises from the deep emotions that hold him in their strong grip, not from churlishness.

"And now," observes Mr. Hewes, who is thinking only of heaping extra honor on his young friend, "since we have a fully commissioned officer to perform the ceremony, suppose we make memorable the day by going down to the Alfred and 'breaking out' its pennant. Thus, almost with the breath in which we commission our first officer, we will have also commissioned our first regular ship of war."

"Would it not be better," interposes Mr. Hancock, thinking on the possible angers of Mr. Adams, "to wait for the coming from Boston of Captain Saltonstall?"

Mr. Hewes thinks it would not. Since Mr. Hewes' manner in thus thinking is just a trifle iron-bound, not to say acrid, Mr. Hancock decides that, after all, there may be more peril in waiting for Captain Saltonstall than in going forward with Lieutenant Jones. Whereupon, Mr. Hewes, Mr. Hancock and Lieutenant Jones depart for the Alfred, which lies at the foot of Chestnut Street. In the main hall of Congress the three pick up Colonel Carroll, Mad Anthony Wayne. Mr. Jefferson, Mr. Livingston, and Mr. Morris. These gentlemen, regarding the event as the formal birth of the new navy, decide to accompany the others in the rôle of witnesses.

The flag is ready in the lockers of the Alfred—a pine tree, a rattlesnake, with the words "Don't Tread on Me." Lieutenant Paul Jones, as he shakes out the bunting, surveys the device with no favoring eye.

The flag is bent on the halyards and "broken out."
Page 100.

"I was ever," observes Lieutenant Paul Jones, looking at Mr. Hewes but speaking to all—"I was ever curious to know by whose queer fancy that device was adopted. It is beyond me to fathom how a venomous serpent could be regarded as the emblem of a brave and honest people fighting to be free."

After delivering this opinion, which is tacitly agreed to by the others, the flag is bent on the halyards, and "broken out." Also, a ration of grog is issued to the crew—so far as the Alfred is blessed with a crew—by way of fixing the momentous occasion in the forecastle mind. The crew cheers; but whether the cheers are for the grog, or Lieutenant Paul Jones who orders it, or the rattlesnake pine tree ensign that causes the order, no one may say.

Following the "breaking out," the grog and the cheers, Mr. Hewes, Mr. Hancock and their fellow-statesmen, retire—the day being over cold—to the land, while Lieutenant Paul Jones, now and until the coming of Captain Saltonstall in command of the Alfred, remains aboard to take up his duty as a regularly commissioned officer in the regular navy of the colonies.

CHAPTER IX
THE CRUISE OF THE "PROVIDENCE"

Four ships—the Alfred, Captain Saltonstall, in the van, with Commodore Hopkins in command of the squadron—sail away on a rainy February day. They clear Cape Henlopen, and turn their untried prows south by east half south. The fell purpose of Commodore Hopkins is to harry the Bahamas.

It will be nowhere written that Commodore Hopkins, in his designs upon the Bahamas, in any degree succeeds. Eight weeks later, the four ships come scudding into New London with the fear of death in their hearts. An English sloop of war darted upon them, they say, off the eastern end of Long Island, and they escaped by the paint on their planks.

Lieutenant Paul Jones of the Alfred is afire with anger and chagrin at the miserable failure of the cruise, and goes furiously ashore, nursing a purpose of charging both Commodore Hopkins and Captain Saltonstall with every maritime offence, from sea-idiocy to cowardice. He is cooled off by older and more prudent heads. Also, Commodore Hopkins is summarily dismissed by Congress, while Captain Saltonstall takes refuge behind the broad skirts of his patron Mr. Adams. Thus, that first luckless cruise of the infant navy, conceived in ignorance and in politics brought forth, achieves its dismal finale in investigations, votes of censure, and dismissals, a situation which goes far to justify those December prophecies of Lieutenant Paul Jones, that Mr. Adams, by his selections for commodore and captains, arranged for more courts-martial than victories.

It has one excellent result, however; it teaches Congress to give Lieutenant Paul Jones the sloop Providence, and send him to sea with a command of his own. With him go his faithful blacks, Scipio and Cato; also, as "port-fire," a red Indian of the Narragansett tribe, one Anthony Jeremiah of Martha's Vineyard.

The little sloop—about as big as a gentleman's yacht, she is—clears on a brilliant day in June. For weeks she ranges from Newfoundland to the Bermudas—seas sown with English ships of war. Boatswain Jack Robinson holds this converse with Polly his virtuous wife, when the Providence again gets its anchors down in friendly Yankee mud.

"And what did you do, Jack?" demands wife Polly, now she has him safe ashore.

"I'll tell you what he—that's the captain—does, when first we puts to sea. He's only a leftenant—Leftenant Paul Jones; but he ought to be a captain, and so, d'ye see, my girl, I'll call him captain. What does the captain do, says you, when once he's afloat? As sure as you're on my knee, Polly, no sooner be we off soundings than he passes the word for'ard for me to fetch him the cat-o'-nine-tails—me being bo'sen. Aft I tumbles, cat and all, wondering who's to have the dozen.

"'Chuck it overboard, Jack!' says he, like that.

"'Chuck what, capt'n?' says I, giving my forelock a tug.

"'Chuck the cat!' says he.

"'The cat?' says I, being as you might say taken a-back, and wondering is it rum.

"'Ay! the cat!' he says. Then, looking me over with an eye like a coal, he goes on: 'I can keep order aboard my ship without the cat. Because why; because I'm the best man aboard her,' he says; and there you be."

"And did the cat go overboard, Jack?"

"Overboard of course, Polly. And being nicely fitted with little knobs of lead on the nine tails of her, down to the bottom like a solid shot goes she. And so, d'ye see, we goes cruising without the cat."

"Did you take no prizes?"

"We sunk eight, and sent eight more into Boston with prize crews aboard. Good picking, too, they was."

"And you had no battles then?"

"No battles, Polly; and yet, at the close of the cruise, we're all but done for by a seventy-four gun frigate off Montauk. The captain twists us out of the frigate's mouth by sheer seamanship."

"Now how was that, Jack!" cries Polly, breathless and all ears.

"We comes poking 'round the point, d'ye see, and runs blind into her. We beats to wind'ard; so does the frigate. And she lays as close to the wind as we—and closer, Polly. Just as she thinks she has only to reach out and snap us up, the captain—he has the wheel himself—wears suddenly round under easy helm, and gets the wind free. This sort o' takes the frigate by surprise, and, instead of wearing, she starts to box about. She's standing as close-hauled as her trim will bear at the time. So, as I says, as he wears 'round, the frigate jams her helm down, and luffs into the teeth of the gale. There's a squall cat's-pawing to wind'ard that she ought to have seen, and would if she'd had our captain. But she never notices. So, d'ye see, my girl, the frigate don't hold her luff, and next the squall takes her in the face. She loses her steering way, gets took aback; and we showing a clean pair of heels, with the wind free, on the sloop's best point of sailing. And there you be: We leaves the frigate to clear her sheets and reeve preventers at her leisure—we snapping muskets at her from our taffer-rail, by way of insult, Polly!" "Your captain's too daring, Jack," says Polly, who is a prudent woman.

"That's what I tells him, Polly. 'Cap'n,' says I, 'discretion is the better part of valor.' At that he gives me a wink. 'So it is, my mate,' says he, 'and damned impudence is the better part of discretion. And now,' says he, 'the frigate being all but hulldown astern, you may take this wheel yourself, while I goes down to supper.'" When Lieutenant Paul Jones is again on dry land, he finds two pieces of news awaiting him. One is a letter from Mr. Jefferson, enclosing his commission as a captain fully fledged. The other is old Duncan Macbean in person, and his sunken cheek and leaden eye tell of troubles on the far-off Rappahannock. "It was Lord Dunmore," says old Duncan, very pale, his voice a-quaver. "He heard of you among the ships, and wanted revenge."

"And the villain took it!"

"Ay, he took it like! He burned mansion, barn, flour-mill—every building's gone, and never stick nor stone to stand one a-top t'ither on the whole plantation."

"What else?"

"He killed sheep and swine and cattle, and drove away the horses; there's never the hoof left walking about the place. Nothing but the stripped land is left ye."

"But the slaves?"

"His lordship took them, too, to sell them in Jamaica."

Captain Paul Jones turns white as linen three times bleached. His eyes are hard as jade. Then he tosses up his hands, with a motion of sorrow.

"My poor blacks!" he cries. "The plantation was to them a home, not a place of bondage. Now they are torn away, to die of pestilence or under the lash, in the cane fields of Jamaica. The price of their poor bodies is to swell the pockets of our noble English slave-trader. This may be Lord Dunmore's notion of civilized war. For all that I shall one day exact a reckoning." Then, resting his hand on old Duncan's shoulder: "However, we have seen worse campaigns, old friend! We'll do well yet! I've still one fortune—my sword; still one prospect—the prospect of laying alongside the enemy."

CHAPTER X
THE COUNSEL OF CADWALADER

Philadelphia is experiencing a cool June, and in a sober, Quakerish way shows grateful for it. The windows of General Washington's apartments, looking out into Chestnut Street, are raised to let in the weather and the urbane sun, not too hot, not too cool, casts a slanting glance into the room, as though moved of a solar curiosity concerning the mighty one who inhabits them. The sun, doubtless, goes his way fully satisfied; General Washington himself is there, in casual talk with the Marquis de Lafayette.

There is a marked difference between the General and the Marquis; the former tall, powerful, indomitable—the type American; the latter nervous, optimistic, full of romantic heroisms—the type French. The General is speaking; his manner a model of the courteous and the suave. For the young Marquis is a peer of France, the head of a party, and may be held as carrying at his heels a third of French sentiment and French influence. It is not what he brings, but what he leaves behind him, that makes the young Marquis important.

The talk between the General and the Marquis is running on Captain Paul Jones.

"It surprises me," the General is saying, "it surprises me, my dear Marquis, to learn that you know Captain Jones."

"We meet—Captaine Jones and I," responds Lafayette, in a choppy, fervent fashion of English, that carries something more than a mere flavor of Paris, "we meet, my dear General, in Alexandria by the Potomac, when I come North from the Carolina, where I disbark. Captaine Jones he assist in Alexandria to find horses to bring me here."

"And you believe, as does he, that a best use that can be made of him is to give him a ship, and send him to Europe?"

"Certaine, General, certaine! Give him a good ship, and let him hawk at England with it. It should be a quick, smart ship, that they may not catch him. Give him such a vessel, General, and he will keep five hundred English boats at home to guard the British coasts."

"You think, Marquis, that he would make a good impression in France?"

"The best, General; the best! Captaine Jones has—what you call?—the aplomb, yes, and the grace, the charm, the dash to captivate the fancy of my countrymen—ever brave, the French, they love a brave man like Captaine

Jones! More, General, he speaks the French language, and that is most important."

General Washington stalks up and down the polished, hardwood floor, wearing a thoughtful face. As he turns to speak, he is interrupted by an obsequious black attendant—one of those body slaves brought from Mount Vernon.

"Pardon, Gin'ral," says the grizzled old darky, as he pokes his grinning head in at the door; "Cap'n Jones presents his comp'ments, sare; an' can he come up?"

General Washington makes a sign of assent, and the grizzled old servitor smirks and smiles and bows himself backward into the hall.

There are two pairs of feet heard climbing the stair; the elastic step belongs to Captain Paul Jones, the more stolid is that of Mr. Morris, who, using the familiarity of a closest friendship, walks in on General Washington unannounced.

"The Marquis was just saying," observes General Washington to Captain Paul Jones, when greetings are over and conversation, to employ a nautical phrase, has settled to its lines, "that he met you in Virginia as he came up."

"Yes, General; I had been having a look at my plantation, which Lord Dunmore did me the honor to lay waste."

"Was the destruction great?"

"The torch had been everywhere. The work could not have been more complete had his Lordship been a professional incendiary." Captain Paul Jones shrugs his wide shoulders, as though dismissing a disagreeable subject, one not to be helped by talk: "You received my letter, General? I was so rash as to think you might aid me in getting the new frigate Trumbull."

"Captain," returns General Washington, "you will understand that my connection with the army makes any interference on my part in naval affairs a most delicate business. I must give my counsel in that quarter cautiously. As for the Trumbull; it is, I fear, already claimed by Mr. Adams for Captain Saltonstall."

"Captain Saltonstall!" cries Captain Paul Jones in a fervor of bitterness. "General, hear me! I sailed lieutenant in the Alfred with Captain Saltonstall. I know him, and do not scruple to say that he is an incompetent coward. Since he went ashore in New London after that disgraceful cruise, he hasn't shown his face aboard ship. He was ashamed to do so. Only Mr. Adams could have protected him from the court-martial he had earned. On my side—if I must plead my own cause—I've made two cruises since then, one in the Providence, one in the Alfred. I've taken twenty-four prizes; some of them by no means unimportant to the American cause."

"Ah, yes!" interrupts General Washington, his steady face lighting up a trifle; "you mean the Mellish and the Bideford. I heard how you captured the winter equipment meant for Howe's army—ten thousand uniforms, eleven hundred fur overcoats, eleven thousand blankets, besides a battery or two of field guns and six hundred cavalry equipments. You did us a timely service, Captain Jones. Many an American soldier was the warmer last winter, because of the Mellish and the Bideford."

"I am glad," says Captain Paul Jones, not without confusion, "to learn that I so much pleased you. It gives me courage to hope that you will come to my shoulder against Mr. Adams and his pet incompetent, Saltonstall."

General Washington again dons his manner of grave inscrutability, and falls to his habit of striding up and down, hands locked beneath the buff-and-blue flaps of his coat.

"Captain Jones," he suddenly breaks forth, "you are a sailor: What do you do afloat in case of a head wind!"

"A head wind?" repeats Captain Paul Jones. "Why, sir, if it's no more than just a gale, I fall to tacking, sta'board and port. If it should be aught of a hurricane, now, I'd set a storm stays'l, heave to, and wait for weather."

"Quite so!" returns the General, soberly. "Well, Captain Jones, one may find headwinds ashore as well as afloat. Now, in the matter of the Trumbull, I should advise you to 'heave to,' as you say, 'and wait for weather.' Mr. Adams insists on Captain Saltonstall; and it is not alone inconvenient, it's impossible, with the Marine Committee made up as it is, to oppose him. Be patient, and you shall not in the end fare worse than your deserts."

Captain Paul Jones wheels on Mr. Morris, who, with Lafayette, has kept silence, while giving interested ear to the conversation.

"You hear, Mr. Morris?" observes Captain Paul Jones, manner dogged and aggressive. "As I warned you in my letter, I shall now prefer charges against Captain Saltonstall—charge him with flat cowardice while in command of the Alfred, and demand a court-martial. Under the circumstances, I deem it my public duty so to do."

Mr. Morris makes a gesture of dissent and repressive protest.

"My dear Captain," expostulates Mr. Morris, his manner pleading, yet full of authority; precisely the manner of one who deals with a trained tiger which he is willing to coax, while firmly intending to control—"my dear Captain, hear reason! Your charges would be suppressed—pigeon-holed! The influence of Mr. Adams with the Marine Committee is supreme. It could, let me tell you, accomplish much more than merely silence your charges. It could go further, and force a resolution of confidence in Captain Salton-stall."

"Then," retorts Captain Paul Jones, inveterate as iron, "I've still a shot in my locker. I shall publish his cowardice over my own name; I shall placard every street corner; for I think the American people entitled to know the sort of servant they have had in Captain Saltonstall. They shall not risk a good ship and a brave crew, with a coward in the dark; and so I tell you!"

"Captain Jones," observes General Washington, who, cool and unruffled, is a contrast to the disturbed Mr. Morris, "Captain Jones, as a gentleman, you realize what would be the result of a public charge of cowardice against Captain Saltonstall?"

"He would challenge you instantly!" breaks in Mr. Morris.

"Precisely!" says Captain Paul Jones, with just the preliminary glimmer of battle in his hard brown eyes. "As you say, sir, he would challenge me. And having challenged me, I should take pleasure in doing my best to kill him. I got a pair of Galway duelling pistols out of the Bideford; they were coming to Lord Howe. If I can lure Captain Saltonstall to the field, it shall go hard, but with one of those Irish sawhandles I rid the American navy of him. Once I have him at ten paces, it will take something more than the influence of Mr. Adams to bring him safely off."

Mr. Morris' brow colors; General Washington takes the situation more at ease. He even gives way briefly to a shadowy smile; for the great patriot, while not so inflammable, is quite as combative as any Captain Paul Jones of them all.

"You have taken advice on this?" asks General Washington, following a pause, during which everybody has had time to more or less digest Captain Paul Jones' unique plan for improving the American navy. "I do not suppose you have gone to this decision without counsel?"

"Sir; I am, as you know, both prudent and conservative—no one more so. Certainly, I've taken counsel. I went to General Cadwalader; he expresses himself as in hearty accord with me. Indeed, it is understood between us that he shall act for me in any affair I may have with Captain Saltonstall."

At the mention of General Cadwalader, General Washington smiles openly, while Mr. Morris groans and throws up his hands.

"Bless me! Cadwalader!" exclaims Mr. Morris, when he can command his tongue. "The worst firebrand in the country! Cadwalader, forsooth! who has ever had but one word of advice for every man—'Fight!'" Then, abruptly descending upon Captain Paul Jones with all the authority of a father addressing a favorite but rebellious son: "Paul; listen! You believe me your friend?"

"Indubitably! I have no better friend."

"Then let me tell you, Paul: In the name of that friendship this thing must end—absolutely end. If you've drawn up any accusation of cowardice against Captain Saltonstall, you must burn it and forget the whole affair. You must dismiss this subject from your mind. In Cadwalader you have invited the wrong kind of advice. I now give you the right kind. The General will tell you so; your friend, the Marquis, will tell you so. And forasmuch as you value my friendship you must obey me."

Mr. Morris in his earnestness lays a paternal hand on the shoulder of Captain Paul Jones, his manner a composite of coax and command. Before the latter, who is visibly shaken by the friendly determination of Mr. Morris, can frame reply, Lafayette—who has been scrupulous to maintain a polite silence from first to last—interferes.

"Our good friend, Mr. Morris," interjects Lafayette, "has been so generous as to refer to me. I could not have said a word without; since what you discuss is private and personal to yourselves as Americans, and of a character that forbids me, a Frenchman and an alien even though a friend, voicing my views. However, since Mr. Morris has so complimented me as to make his appeal in my name, I must—in all respect and friendship for Captain Jones, whom I admire—unite my voice with his. The more readily since I can take it upon myself to promise Captain Jones that if he will cross to France, with a letter I shall give him to my king, a fighting ship of frigate strength shall be his within the month."

As he concludes, Lafayette, a blush reddening his cheek—for he is only a boy—extends two hands to Captain Paul Jones as though, fearful of having said too much, he would mutely apologize. Captain Paul Jones seizes the hands with a warmth equal to the other's; and the incident, capping as it does the fatherly opposition of Mr. Morris, puts an end to that beautiful plan, so full of dire promise for Captain Saltonstall, which in their mutual belligerencies Captain Paul Jones and the fire-fed Cadwalader have formulated.

"Say that you will go to France, my friend!" urges the impulsive young Frenchman; "say that you will go! I will exhaust Auvergne, and all of France besides, but you shall have the promised ship."

At this, General Washington interferes.

"Forbear, my dear Marquis!" says he. "Captain Jones shall go to France. But he shall go with an American crew, in an American ship, flying the American flag." Then, to Captain Paul Jones: "Do me the honor, Captain, to hold yourself in readiness to obey any summons I may send. Believe me, I shall count myself as one without influence, if you do not hear from me within the week."

Let us glance ahead two years for the final word of Captain Saltonstall. Captain Paul Jones, with his hard-won prize, the crippled Serapis, creeps into the Texel, and the earliest story wherewith the Dutch regale him is how Captain Saltonstall, weak, forceless, incompetent, has surrendered the new, thirty-two-gun frigate, Warren, to the English in Penobscot Bay. Captain Paul Jones hears the disgraceful news with set and angry face.

"I have just learned the miserable fate of the Warren," he writes to Mr. Morris; "and hearing it I reproach myself. If I had obeyed the dictates of my sense of duty on a Philadelphia day you will recall, instead of yielding to the persuasions of the peacemakers, our flag might still be flying on the Warren!"

CHAPTER XI
THE GOOD SHIP RANGER

Four days of listless waiting go by, and Captain Paul Jones again finds himself and Mr. Morris closeted with General Washington.

"Captain Jones," says the latter, speaking with a kindly gravity, "Mr. Morris and I have so pushed your affairs with the Marine Committee that to-morrow Congress will pass a double resolution, adopting a new flag, the stars and stripes, and appointing you to command the Ranger."

"The Ranger!" exclaims Captain Paul Jones, beginning to glow. "Thanks, General; a thousand thanks! And to you also, Mr. Morris, whom I shall never forget! The Ranger! I know her! She is being sparred and rigged at Portsmouth! New, three hundred tons; a beauty, too, they tell me! Gentlemen, I am off at once to Portsmouth! I must see to stepping her masts and mounting her batteries myself."

Captain Paul Jones, all eagerness, is on his feet, and even the wise, age-cold Mr. Morris begins to catch his fire.

"Right!" cries Mr. Morris; "you shall start to-morrow!"

"Captain Jones," interrupts the General, laying a large detaining hand on the other's arm, "you will go to Portsmouth and look after your ship. Also, while your destination is France, you must wait for orders to sail. I may have weighty despatches for the French King—news that will shake Europe."

June is as cool in Portsmouth as it is in Philadelphia. Cooler; for the New Hampshire breeze has in it the chill smell of those snows that lie unmelted in the mountains. Captain Paul Jones comes unannounced, eyes dancing like those of a child with a new toy, and seeks the wharf where the __Ranger__ is being fitted to her spars. From a convenient coign he looks the Ranger over, and evinces a master's appreciation.

"Nose sharp! Plenty of dead-rise! Lean lines!" he murmurs. "With the wind anywhere abaft the beam, she should race like a greyhound! All, she's a beauty, fit to warm the cockles of a sailor's heart! See to the sheer of her!—as delicate as the lines of a woman's arm!"

Up comes a sturdy figure with an air of command, an officer's hat on his head, a ship-carpenter's adz in his hand.

"This is Captain Jones?"

"Captain Paul Jones, sir."

"Pardon me for not first giving my name. I'm Elijah Hall, who is to sail second officer with you in yon Ranger."

Captain Paul Jones and Lieutenant Hall fall into instant and profound confab of a deeply nautical complexion, a confab quite beyond a landsman's comprehension, wherein such phrases as "flush-decks," "short poop-deck," "bilges," "futtocks," and "knees" abound, and are reeled off as though their use gives our two ship-enthusiasts unbridled satisfaction. At last Lieutenant Hall remarks, pointing to three long sticks:

"There're her masts, sir. They were taken out of a four-hundred-ton Indiaman, and are too long for a three-hundred-ton ship like the Ranger. I was thinking I'd cut'em off four feet in the caps."

"That would be a sin!" exclaims Captain Paul Jones, voice almost religious in its fervent zeal. "Three as fine pieces of pine as ever came out of Norway, too! I'd be afraid to cut'em, Mr. Hall; it would give the ship bad luck. I'll tell you what! Fid them four feet lower in the hounds; it will amount to the same thing, and at the same time save the sticks."

Captain Paul Jones goes at the congenial task of fitting out the Ranger with his usual day-and-night energy. When he finds her over-sparred, with her masts too long, he still refuses to cut them down, but shortens yard and bowsprit, jib-boom and spankerboom. He doesn't like the Marine Committee's armament of twenty six-pounders, and proceeds to mount four six-pounders and fourteen long nines.

"One nine-pounder is equal to two six-pounders," says Captain Paul Jones; "and, since it's I who must put to sea in the Ranger, and not the Marine Committee, nine-ponnders I'll have, and say no more about it."

The New Hampshire girls, on the Fourth of July, come down to the Ranger, and present Captain Paul Jones a flag—red, white, and blue—quilted of cloth ravished from their virgin petticoats. The gallant mariner makes the New Hampshire girls a speech.

"That flag," cries he, "that flag and I, as captain of the Ranger, were born on the same day. We are twins. We shall not be parted life or death; we shall float together or sink together!"

These brave words, in the long run, find amendment. The petticoat flag of the pretty New Hampshire girls is the flag which, two years later, flies from the Richard's indomitable peak when Captain Paul Jones cuts down the gallant Pierson and his Serapis. After that fight off Scarborough Head, Captain Paul Jones writes to the pretty New Hampshire girls—for he ever remembers the ladies—recounting the last destiny of their petticoat ensign. He is telling of the Richard's death throes, as viewed from the blood-slippery decks of the conquered Serapis:

"No one was now left aboard the Richard but my dead. To them I gave the good old ship to be their coffin; in her they found a sublime sepulcher. She rolled heavily in the swell, her gun-deck awash to the port-sills, settled slowly by the head, and sank from sight. The ensign gaff, shot away in the action, had been fished and put in place; and there your flag was left flying when we abandoned her. As she went down by the head, her taffrail rose for a moment; and so the last that mortal eye ever saw of the gallant Richard was your unconquered ensign. I couldn't strip it from the brave old ship in her last agony; nor could I deny my dead on her decks, who had given their lives to keep it flying, the glory of taking it with them. And so I parted with it; so they took it for their winding sheet."

At last the Ranger is ready for sea; and still those belated despatches from General Washington for the French King do not come. One cold October day a horseman, worn and haggard, rides into Portsmouth. Stained, dust-caked, reeling in his saddle, he calls for Captain Paul Jones.

"Here," responds that gentleman. "What would you have?"

"I come from General Washington," cries the man. "Burgoyne has surrendered! Here are your despatches for France!"

Captain Paul Jones takes the packet, stunned for the moment by the mighty news.

"And now for food and drink," says the man faintly, as with difficulty he slips to the ground. "One hundred and eighty miles have I rode in thirty hours. It was the brave news kept me going; the thought of those beaten English held me up like wine."

"One hundred and eighty miles!" cries Captain Paul Jones. "Thirty hours!"

The man points to his mount, where it stands with drooping head and quivering flank.

"That is the tenth I've had. Horse flesh and hard riding did it!"

Ten minutes after the despatches are put in his hands, Captain Paul Jones is aboard the Ranger. Then comes the tramp of forty feet about the capstan. Twenty powerful breasts are pressed against the capstan bars, and the Ranger is walked up to its anchors, while aloft the brisk top-men are shaking out the sails.

"Anchor up and down, sir!" reports Boatswain Jack Robinson, who has left his Polly at home, while he sails with the Ranger.

"Anchor up and down!" repeats Captain Paul Jones. "Bring her home!"

With a "Heave ho!" the Ranger's anchors are pulled out of Portsmouth sands. Captain Paul Jones himself takes the wheel and pays off its head before the breeze, already bellying the foresails.

"Give her every stitch you have, Mr. Hall," says Captain Paul Jones. "We must be clear of the Isles of Shoals by daybreak."

"And then?" asks Lieutenant Hall.

"East, by south, half east! And Mr. Hall, day and night, blow high, blow low, spread every rag you've got. Burgoyne has surrendered. Either I shall tear the sticks out of the Ranger, or spread that news in France in thirty days."

"More haste, less speed!" murmurs the prudent Lieutenant Hall; and so, having eased his mind like a true seaman, he goes forward heatedly to spread sail.

The top-heavy little Ranger, with her acre of canvas, heels over until, with decks awash, she glides eastward like a ghost.

"Pipe all hands aft, Mr. Bo'sen!" commands Captain Paul Jones.

Boatswain Jack Robinson puts his whistle to his lips, and sends a shrill call singing through the ship. The crew come scampering aft; all save a contingent aloft, who race down by the backstays, claw under claw, as might so many cats. Some of our old friends of the Providence are there— the aquatic Scipio and Cato, with the little red Indian port-fire, Anthony Jeremiah.

"My men," cries Captain Paul Jones, "we're off for France. We shall meet nasty weather, for it's the beginning of winter, and I shall steer the northern course. It is to be a case of crack-on canvas, foul weather or fair: and, since the ship is oversparred and cranky, we must mind her day and night. To make all safe, the watch shall be lap-watched, so as to keep plenty of hands on deck. This will double your work, but I shall also double your grog. Now, my hearties, let every man among you do his duty by flag and ship. Burgoyne has surrendered, and it's for us to carry the word to France."

"Shipmates," observes Boatswain Jack Robinson, judgmatically, as the hands go tumbling forward, "shipmates, the old Ranger is a damned comfortable ship. 'Double watches, double work!' says the skipper; but also 'Double grog!' says he. Wherefore, I says again, the old Ranger is a damned comfortable ship."

Eight bells now, breakfast; and the Isles of Shoals are vanishing over the Ranger's stern. Suddenly a boyish voice strikes up:

"So now we had him hard and fast,

Burgoyne laid down his arms at last,

And that is why we brave the blast,

To carry the news to France."

Captain Paul Jones pauses in his short quarterdeck walk, cocks his ear, and listens. The hoarse crew take up the chorus:

"Heigh ho! carry the news!

Go carry the news to London,

Tell old King George how he's undone.

Oh, ho! carry the news!"

Boatswain Jack Robinson, observing Captain Paul Jones listening, becomes explanatory.

"Only a bit of a ditty, Cap'n; the same composed by Midshipman Hill, d'ye see, in honor of this here cruise. A right good ballid, too, I calls it; and amazin' fine for a lad of twenty, who hardly knows a reef-point from a gasket."

Vouchsafing this, Boatswain Jack Robinson rolls forward with walrus gait, chanting as he goes in a voice tuned by storms and broken across capstan bars, the hoarse refrain:

"Oh, ho! carry the news!"

And so the good ship Ranger plows eastward on her course. Eighteen hours out of twenty-four, Captain Paul Jones holds the deck. In the end he has his reward. Just thirty days after the Ranger's anchors kissed the Portsmouth sands good-by, they go splashing into the dull waters of the Loire.

CHAPTER XII
HOW THE "RANGER" TOOK THE "DRAKE"

Four months slip by; it is April, and the idle Ranger rides in the harbor of Brest. Morose, sore with inactivity, Captain Paul Jones seeks out Doctor Franklin at the philosopher's house in Passy.

"This lying by rusts me," Captain Paul Jones is saying as he and Doctor Franklin have a turn in the garden. The latter likes the thin French sunshine, and gets as much of it as he may. "Yes, it rusts me—fills me with despair!"

"What would you do, then?" asks Doctor Franklin, his coarse, shrewd face quickening into interest. "Have you a cruise mapped out?"

"Now I thought, if you've no objections, I'd just poke the Ranger's nose into the Irish Sea, and take a look at Whitehaven. You know I was born by the Solway, and the coast I speak of is an old acquaintance."

"I see no objection, Captain, save the smallness of your ship."

"That is easily answered; for I give you my word, Doctor, the little Ranger can sail round any English ship on the home station. I shall be safe, no fear; for what I can't whip I can run from."

"Have you spoken to my brother commissioners?"

Doctor Franklin looks up, a grim, expectant twinkle in his gray eyes. Captain Paul Jones cracks his fingers in angry impatience.

"Forgive me, Doctor, if I'm frank to the frontiers of rudeness. Of what avail to speak to Mr. Dean, who is asleep? Of what avail to speak to Mr. Lee, who surrounds himself with British spies like that creature Thornton, his private secretary? I ask you plain questions, Doctor, for I know you to be a practical man."

The philosopher grins knowingly.

"Please do not speak of British spies to Commissioner Lee, Captain Jones. My task in France is enough difficult as it stands."

"And on that account, Doctor, and on that alone, I have so far refrained from saying aught to Mr. Lee. But I tell you I misdoubt the man. His fellow Thornton I know to be in daily communication with the English admiralty! he clinks English gold in his pockets as the wage of his treason. This, were there no one save myself to consider, I should say in the face of Arthur

Lee; ay! for that matter in the face of all the Lees that ever hailed from Virginia. I tell you this, Doctor, for your own guidance." Then, following a pause: "Not that it sets politely with my years to go cautioning one so much my superior in age, wisdom and experience."

The philosopher glances up from the violets.

"Possibly, Captain Jones, I have already given myself that caution. However, concerning your proposed cruise: I shall leave all to your judgment. Certainly, our warships, as you say, were meant for battle-work, and not to waste their lives junketing about French ports."

"One thing, doctor," observes Captain Paul Jones, at parting: "Tell your fellow commissioners that I've cleared for the west coast of Ireland, with a purpose to go north-about around the British islands. If you let them hear I'm off for Whitehaven, I give you my honor that, with the spy Thornton selling my blood to the English admiralty, I shall have the whole British fleet at my heels before I reach St. George's Channel."

Captain Paul Jones, in command of the Ranger, drops in at Whitehaven. With twenty-nine of his lads he goes ashore of a dripping morning, pens up the sleepy garrisons of the two forts, and spikes their guns. Then, having spikes to spare, he makes useless a shore battery, while the ballad-mongering Midshipman Hill, with six men, chases inland one hundred coast guardsmen and militia.

Captain Paul Jones, waxing industrious, attempts to burn the shipping which crowds the tidal basin at Whitehaven. In these fire-lighting efforts he succeeds to the extent of five ships; after which he rows out to the Ranger. Thereupon the people and militia, who crowd the terror-smitten hills round about, come down into their town again.

Captain Paul Jones crosses now to the north shore of the Solway for a morning call upon the Earl of Selkirk. He schemes to capture that patrician, and trade him back to the English for certain good American sailors whom they hold as prisoners. The plan falls through, since the noble earl is not at home. In lieu, the Ranger's crew take unto themselves the Selkirk plate, which Captain Paul Jones subsequently buys from them, paying the ransom from his own purse, and returns with his compliments gallantly expressed in a letter to the earl.

From the Solway, the little Ranger stands west by north across the Irish Sea. Off Carrickfergus she finds the Drake, an English sloop of war that is two long nines the better than the Ranger in her broadsides, and thirty-one men stronger in her crew. To save trouble, the Ranger is hove to off the mouth of Belfast Lough, and waits for the Drake to come out. This the English ship does slowly and with difficulty, being on the wrong side of wind and tide.

"The sun is no more than an hour high,"

The Story of Paul Jones suggests Lieutenant Wallingford wistfully. "Shouldn't we go to meet them, sir?"

Captain Paul Jones shakes his head.

"We've better water here," says he. "Besides, the moon will be big; we'll fight them by the light of the moon."

Slowly, reluctantly, the Drake forges within hail. She is in doubt about the Ranger.

"What ship is that?" cries the Drake.

Captain Paul Jones puts his speaking-trumpet to his lips.

"The American ship Ranger," he replies. "Come on; we're waiting for you."

Without further parley, broadside answers broadside and the battle is on.

Both ships head north, the Ranger having the weather-gage. This last gives Captain Paul Jones the nautical upperhand. In ship-fighting, the weather-gage is equivalent to an underhold in wrestling.

There is a swell on, and the two ships roll heavily. They shape their course side by side, keeping within musket-reach of each other. The breeze is on the starboard quarter, and a little faster than the ships. By this good luck, the smoke of the broadsides is sent drifting ahead, and the line of sight between the ships kept free. On they crawl, broadside talking to broadside; only the Americans are smarter with their guns, and fire three to the Drake's two.

Twilight now invests the scene in gray, as the sun sinks behind the close, dark Irish headlands to the west. Night, cloudless and serene, comes down; the round, full moon shines out, and its mild rays mingle and merge with the angry glare of the battle-lanterns. Captain Paul Jones from his narrow quarterdeck watches the Drake through his night glass.

"Good! Very good!" he murmurs, as the Drake's foremast is splintered by a round shot. Then, to the Salem man who has the wheel: "Bring us a little closer, Mr. Sargent; a little closer in, if you please."

Captain Paul Jones again rivets his glass upon the Drake. An exclamation escapes him. It comes upon him that his gunners are having advantage of the roll of the ships, and time their broadsides so as to catch the Drake as, reeling to port, she brings up her starboard side. By this plausible manouvre, those sagacious ones who train the Ranger's guns are sending shot after shot through and through the Drake, between wind and water, half of them indeed below the water-line. Captain Paul Jones, through his glass, makes out the black round shot-holes; they show as thick as cloves in the rind of a Christmas ham.

"Why!" he exclaims, "this doesn't match my book! I must put a stopper on such work."

Shutting up his glass, Captain Paul Jones leaps from the after flush-deck down among his sailors. Drunk with blood, grimed of powder, naked to the waist, the black glory of battle in their hearts, they merrily work their guns. It is as he beheld from the after-deck. The Ranger rolls to port as the Drake, all dripping, is fetching up her starboard side.

"Fire!" cries the master-gunner, and "Fire!" runs the word along the battery.

The long nines respond with flame and bellow!

Then they race crashingly inboard with the recoil, and are caught by the breeching tackle. With that the smoky work is all to do over again. The brawny sailor men—from Nantucket, from Martha's Vineyard, from Sag Harbor, from New London and Barnstable and Salem and Boston and Portsmouth they are—shirtless and shoeless, barefoot and stripped to the belts, ply sponge and rammer. Again each black-throated gun is ready with a stomachful of solid shot.

"Show 'em your teeth, mates!"

The guns rattle forward on their carriages. The quick port-tires stand ready, blowing their matches. There is a brief pause, as the master-gunner waits for that fatal downward roll to port which offers and opens the Drake's starboard side almost to the keel.

"Ah! I see, Mr. Starbuck," begins Captain Paul Jones sweetly, addressing the master-gunner. "Your effort is to hull the enemy."

"Fire!" cries the master-gunner, for just then the Ranger is reeling down to port, while the Drake is coming up to starboard, and he must not waste the opportunity.

The long nines roar cheerfully, spouting fire and smoke. Then comes that crashing inboard leap, to be caught up short by the tackle. Again the sponges; again the rammers; with the busy shot-handlers working in between. And all the while the little powder monkeys, lads of eleven and twelve, go pattering to and fro, with cartridges from the magazines.

"Why, yes, sir!" responds the master-gunner, now finding time to reply to the comment of Captain Paul Jones; "as you says, we're trying to hull her, sir."

Captain Paul Jones makes out three new holes below the Brake's plankslieer, the hopeful harvest of that last broadside.

"May I ask," demands Captain Paul Jones, who as a mere first effect of battle never fails of a rippling amiability, "may I ask, Mr. Starbuck, your design in thus aiming below the water-line?"

"Saving you presence, Captain, we designs to sink the bitch."

"Precisely! That is what I surmised! To a quick seaman like yourself, Mr. Starbuck, a word will do. I don't want her sunk, d'ye see! I want to bring her into France as an object-lesson, and show the Frenchmen what Americans can do. Under the circumstances, Mr. Starbnck, I shall be obliged if you let her hull alone. It will take Mr. Hitchburn, our carpenter, a week as it is "—this comes off reproachfully—"to stop the holes you've already made. And so, Mr. Starbnck, from now on comb her decks and cut her up in the spars as much as ever you like; but please keep off her hull."

"Ay, ay, sir!" says the master-gunner, saluting. Then: "Pass the word that we're to leave her hull alone. Cap'n has set his heart on catching her alive."

With that the plan of attack finds reversal, the Ranger firing as she comes up to port and when only a narrow streak of the Drake's starboard beam is visible above the waves.

Captain Paul Jones remains among the sailors, canvassing in a gratified way the results of this change. While thus engaged, port-fire Anthony Jeremiah grins up at him, meanwhile blowing his match to keep it lighted.

"You enjoy yourself, I see, Jerry," remarks Captain Paul Jones, who, as observed, is never so affable as when guns are crashing, blood is flowing, and splinters flying.

"Me like to hear the big guns talk, Captain," responds the Indian. "It gives Jerry a good heart."

Captain Paul Jones again swings his glass on the Drake. He is just in time to see her fore and main topsail-yards come down onto the caps by the run. The last broadside does that. In an instant, he is running aft.

"Down with your helm, Mr. Sargent!" he roars. "Pull her down for every ounce that's in you, man!"

Quartermaster Sargent, thus encouraged, climbs the wheel like a squirrel; the Ranger's topsails shiver; then, yielding to her helm, she slowly luffs across the helpless stern of the Drake.

"Aboard with those sta'board tacks!" shouts Captain Paul Jones. Then, turning again to the wheelman: "Steady, Mr. Sargent; keep her full!"

There is a skurry across the Ranger's decks, as the men rush from the port to the starboard battery.

"Stand by, Mr. Starbuck," calls ont Captain Paul Jones, "to rake her as we cross her stern."

"Ay, ay, sir!" returns the master-gunner. "She shall have it for'ard and aft, as my old gran'am shells peas cods!"

"Steady, Mr. Sargent!" and again Captain Paul Jones cautions the alert wheelman. "Keep her as she is!"

The guns are swung, and depressed so as to tear the poor Drake open from stern-post to cutwater at one discharge. The Ranger gathers head; slowly she makes ready to cross her enemy's stern so close that one might chuck a biscuit aboard. It is a moment fraught of life and death for the unhappy Drake.

With her captain and first officer already dead, the situation proves beyond the second officer, on whom the responsibility of fighting or surrendering the ship devolves. His sullen British soul gives way; and he strikes his colors just in time to avoid that raking fire which would else have snuffed him off the face of the sea.

"Out-fought, out-manoeuvred, and out-sailed!" exclaims Captain Paul Jones.

Lieutenant Hall, flushed of combat, comes up.

"We have beaten them, Captain!" exults Lieutenant Hall.

"We've done more than that, Mr. Hall," responds Captain Paul Jones. "We have defeated an aphorism, and made a precedent. For the first time in the history of the sea, a lighter ship, with a smaller crew and a weaker battery, has whipped an Englishman."

CHAPTER XIII
THE DUCHESS OF CHARTRES

It is a notable gathering that assembles at Doctor Franklin's house in Passy. Mr. Adams and his wife have just arrived, and the doctor presents them to Madame Brillon and Madame Houdetot, already there.

"Mr. Adams is but recently come from America," the doctor whispers. "He takes Mr. Dean's place as a member of our commission."

Madame Houdetot talks with Mrs. Adams; and because of her bad English and the other's bad French they get on badly.

"Mr. Lee sends his compliments," observes Mr. Adams, loftily, to Doctor Franklin, "and regrets that he cannot come. He heard, I understand, that Captain Paul Jones is to be here, and does not care to meet him."

"No?" responds the doctor, evincing scanty concern at the failure of Mr. Lee to come. "Now I do not wonder! I hear that Captain Jones thrashed Mr. Lee's secretary in a tavern at Nantes, and our proud Mr. Lee, I suppose, resents it."

"Thrashed him!" exclaims Mr. Adams, in high tones; "Captain Jones seized a stick and beat him like a dog, applying to him the while such epithets as 'liar!' and 'spy.' Mr. Lee's secretary has left France through fear of him."

The portly doctor lifts his hands at this; but underneath his deprecatory horror, hides a complacency, a satisfaction, as though the violence of Captain Jones will not leave him utterly unstrung.

"He fights everybody," says the good doctor, resignedly; "on land as well as on sea. Nor can I teach him the difference between his own personal enemies, and the enemies of his country."

"He seems a bit unruly," observes the pompous Mr. Adams; "a bit unruly, does this Captain Jones of yours. I'm told he sold the Drake, and what other ships were captured on his recent cruise, in the most high-handed, masterful way."

"What else was he to do? When a road becomes impassable, what is your course? You push down a panel of fence and go cross-lots. Captain Jones had two hundred prisoners to feed, besides his own brave crew of one hundred and eighteen. We had no money to give him. Were they to starve? I'm not surprised that he sold the ships."

"I'm surprised that the Frenchmen bought them," returns Mr. Adams. "Captain Jones could give no title."

Doctor Franklin's keen eyes twinkle.

"He could give possession, Mr. Adams. And let me tell you that in France, as everywhere else, possession is nine parts of the law."

Madame Brillon draws Mr. Adams aside, while Doctor Franklin welcomes the beautiful royal girl—the Duchess de Chartres; to whom he later presents Mr. Adams and Mrs. Adams. Madame Houdetot leaves Mrs. Adams with the girl-Duchess and talks aside with Doctor Franklin.

"I did not know," she whispers, with an eye on the girlish Duchess, "that you received calls from royalty."

"The Duchess de Chartres has been with her great relative, the king, upon the business of Captain Jones. She comes to meet the captain, whom we every moment expect."

"She is in love with him!—madly in love with him!" says Madame Houdetot. "All the world knows it."

The doctor, who at seventy-two is a distinguished gallant, smiles sympathetically.

"Did I not once tell you that Captain Jones, the invincible among men, is the irresistible among women!"

"Something of the sort, I think. But you have heard of the duchess and your irresistible, invincible one, had you not?"

"My dear madam, I am a diplomat," replies the doctor, slyly. "And it is an infraction of the laws of diplomacy to tell what you hear."

"They have been very tender at the duchess's summer house near Brest."

"And the husband—the Duke de Chartres!"

"A most excellent gentleman! A most admirable husband of most unimpeachable domestic manners! Believe me, I cannot laud him too highly! Every husband in Prance should copy him! He honors his wife, and—stays aboard his ship, the Saint Esprit." After a pause the gossipy Madame Houdetot continues: "No doubt the duke considers his wife's rank. Is the great-granddaughter of the Grande Louis to be held within those narrow lines that confine the feet of other women?"

"Who is this Mr. Adams?" asks Madame Brillon, coming up. "Is he a great man?"

Doctor Franklin glances across where the austere Mr. Adams is stiffly posing, with a final thought of impressing the sparkling Duchess de Chartres.

"Rather he is a big man," replies the philosopher. "Like some houses, his foundations cover a deal of ground; but then he is only one story high. If you could raise Mr. Adams another story, he would be a great man."

The good doctor goes over, and becomes polite to Mrs. Adams; for the enlightenment of that lady of reserve and dignity, he expands on France and the French character. Suddenly the door is thrown open, and all unannounced a queer figure rushes in. She is clad in rumpled muslin and soiled lutestring. Her hair is frizzed, her face painted, her cap awry, and she is fair and fat and of middle years. This remarkable apparition embraces Doctor Franklin, kisses him resoundingly, first on the left cheek then on the right, crying:

"My flame!—my love!—my Franklin!"

The seasoned doctor receives this caressing broadside steadily, while the desolated Mrs. Adams sits round-eyed and stony.

"It is the eccentric Madame Helvetius," explains Madame Brillon in a low tone to Mrs. Adams. "They call her the 'Rich Widow of Passy.' She and the good doctor are dearest friends."

"Eccentric!" Mrs. Adams perceives as much, and says so.

Doctor Franklin returns to Mrs. Adams, whom he suspects of being hungry for an explanation, while the buoyant Madame Helvetius, as one sure of her impregnable position, wanders confidently about the room.

"You should become acquainted with Madame Helvetius," submits the doctor pleasantly. "Wise, generous, afire for our cause—you would dote on her."

Mrs. Adams icily fears not.

"Believe me; you would!" insists the doctor. "True! her manners are of her people and her region. They are not those of Puritan New England."

Mrs. Adams interrupts to say that she has never before heard so much said in favor of Puritan New England.

"And yet, my dear Mrs. Adams," goes on the good doctor, as one determined to conquer for Madame Helvetius the other's favorable opinion, "you would do wrong to apply a New England judgment to our friend. Her exuberance is of the surface." Then, quizzically: "A mere manner, I assure you, and counts for no more than should what she is doing now."

Mrs. Adams lifts her severe gaze at this to Madame Helvetius. That amiable French woman is in rapt and closest converse with Mr. Adams, hand on his shoulder, her widowed lips to his ear. Mr. Adams is standing as one frozen, casting ever and anon a furtive glance, like an alarmed sheep, at Mrs. Adams. For an arctic moment, Mrs. Adams is held by the terrors of that spectacle; then she moves to her husband's rescue.

Madame Helvetius comes presently to Doctor Franklin.

"What an iceberg!" she remarks, with a toss of the frizzed head towards Mr. Adams. "Does he ever thaw!" Then, as her glance takes in Mrs. Adams: "Poor man! He might be August, missing her. It is she who congeals him."

And now he, for whom they wait, is announced—Captain Paul Jones. He has about him everything of the salon and nothing of the sea. His amiable yet polished good breeding wins on Mrs. Adams, and even the repellant wintry Mr. Adams is rendered urbane. Captain Paul Jones becomes the instant centre of the little assemblage. And yet, even while he gives his words to the others, his glances rove softly to the girl-Duchess, who stands apart, as might one who for a space—only for a space—permits room to others. The girl-Duchess is polite; she grants him what time is required to offer his greetings all around. Then, in the most open, obvious way, as though none might criticise or gainsay her conduct, she draws him into a secluded corner. They make a rare study, these two; he deferential yet dominant, she proud but yielding.

"Did you see the king?" he asks.

"See him? Am I not, too, a Bourbon?" This comes off with fire.

"Surely! Of course you saw him!" responds Captain Paul Jones, recalling his manner to one of easy matter-of-fact. "Your royal highness will pardon my inquiry."

The girl-Duchess objects petulantly to the "Royal Highness."

"From you I do not like it," she says. "From you"—and here comes a flood of softness, while her black eyes shine like strange jewels—"from you, as you know, my friend, I would have only those titles that, arm-encircled, heart to heart, a man gives to the one woman of his sou's hope."

Her voice sinks at the close, while her eyes leave his for the floor. His presence is like a gale, and she bends before him as the willow bends before the strong wind. Meanwhile, as instructive to Mr. Adams, the loud Doctor is saying:

"No, sir; you must have a wig. No one sees the king without a wig."

"We talked an hour—the king and I," goes on the girl-Duchess, recovering herself. "I read him your letter; he was vastly interested. Then I told him how the Ranger had been called to America. Also I drew him pictures of what you had done; and how bravely you had fought, not only your enemies, but his enemies and the enemies of France. And, oh!"—here again the black eyes take on that perilous softness—"I can be eloquent when I talk of you!"

Captain Paul Jones looks tender things, as though he also might be eloquent, let him but pick subject and audience. Altogether there is much to support the gossip-loving Madame Houdetot, in what she has said concerning that summer house at Brest. The voice of the good Doctor again takes precedence.

"Until then, it had been an axiom of naval Europe that no one on even terms, guns and men and ship, could whip the British on the ocean."

The Doctor and Mr. Adams are discussing the Ranger and the Drake, a topic that has been rocking France.

"Yes," goes on the girl-Duchess, with a further dulcet flash of those eyes, fed of fire and romance, "you are to have a ship. Here is the king's order to his Minister of Marine—the shuffler De Sartine. Now there shall be no more shuffling." She gives Captain Paul Jones the orders. "The ship is the Duras, lying at l'Orient."

"The Duras!" exclaims Captain Paul Jones. "An ex-Indiaman!—a good ship, too; she mounts forty guns." Then, as his gaze rests on Doctor Franklin, laying down diplomatic law and fact to Mr. Adams, who listens with a preposterously conceited cock to his head: "What say you, my friend—my best, my dearest friend! Let us re-name the Duras for the good Doctor. Shall we not call it the Bon Homme Richard?"

The girl-Duchess looks her acquiescence as she would have looked it to any proposal from so near and sweet and dear a quarter. Thus the Bon Homme Richard is born, and the Duras disappears. The Doctor, unconscious of the honor done him, is saying to Madame Helvetius, whose fat arm is thrown across his philosophic shoulder:

"With pleasure, madam! It is arranged; I shall dine at your house tomorrow."

The girl-Duchess and Captain Paul Jones hear nothing of these prandial arrangements for the morrow. They are again conversing; and, for all they talk constantly, they say more with their eyes than with their lips.

"Lastly," and here the words of the girl-Duchess grow distinct, "your ship, they tell me, will need refitting. That will take money, my friend; and so I hand you this letter to my banker, Gourlade, instructing him to put ten thousand louis to your credit."

Captain Paul Jones puts the letter of credit aside.

"You do not understand!" he says. "De Chaumont has——"

"You must take it!" interrupts the girl-Duchess, her eyes beginning to swim. "You shall not put to sea, and risk your life, and the ship not half prepared!"

"I shall more easily risk my life a thousand times, than permit you to give me money."

As Captain Paul Jones says this, a resentful red is burning on his brow. Doctor Franklin breaks in from over the way, with:

"You should not too much listen to Mr. Lee, sir. I tell you that the French merchants have offered to send Captain Jones to sea as admiral of an entire fleet of privateers, and he refused. Have my word, sir; the last thing he thinks on is money."

The girl-Duchess is gazing reproachfully at Captain Paul Jones. At last she speaks slowly and with a kind of sadness:

"I do not give you money—do not offer it. What! money and—you! Never!" Then proudly: "I give my money to the Cause." After this high note is struck, the flash dies down; the black eyes again go wavering to the floor, while the voice retreats to the old soft whisper. "It is my heart —only my heart that I give to you."

The strident, unmollified tones of Mr. Adams get possession of the field. He is condemning the French press.

"They declare, sir," he is saying, "that I am not the celebrated Mr. Adams; that I am a cipher, a fanatic and a bigot."

Doctor Franklin laughs. "What harm is there in the French papers, sir?" he returns. "Give them no heed, sir, give them no heed!"

Madame Brillon makes preparations to depart; Madame Houdetot, Mrs. Adams and the rest adopt her example. And still the girl-Duchess holds Captain Paul Jones to herself:

"I am to have one evening—one before you go?" she pleads; and her tones are a woman's tones and deeply wistful; and are not in any respect the tones of a Bourbon.

"One evening? You shall have every evening—ay! and every day."

"Remember!" and as she makes ready to go the girl-Duchess takes firmer command of her manner and her voice; "remember! You have promised to lay an English frigate at my feet."

"That I shall do; or lay my bones away in the Atlantic!"

The girl-Duchess shivers at this picture, and as though for reassurance steals her slim hand into his.

"Not that!" she pleads. His strong brown fingers close courageously on the slender ones. "I cannot bear the thought! In victory or defeat, come back!" Then, sighing rather than saying: "Come back to me—my untitled knight of the sea!"

CHAPTER XIV
THE SAILING OF THE "RICHARD"

Captain Paul Jones goes down to l'Orient to begin the overhaul and refit of the Richard. The ship is twenty years old, and he finds it shaken and worn by time and weather. It is not a good ship, not a ship on which a prudent commander would care to stake his life and reputation; but it is the best he can get, and Captain Paul Jones accepts it, shrugging his shoulders. He has been so beaten upon by disappointments, so carked and rusted by delays, since his old ship Ranger spread its sails for home, and left him as it were an exile on French shores, that rather than further endure such heart-eating experiences he is ready to embrace the desperate. As the work of refitting progresses, Doctor Franklin comes over from Passy.

"The ship is old, Doctor," says Captain Paul Jones, as he and Doctor Franklin canvass the situation. "That, however, is the least of my troubles. What causes me most uneasiness is the crew. Out of a whole muster of three hundred and seventy-five, no more than fifty are Americans."

"Then you do not trust the French? Surely you don't mean to say they are not brave men?"

"Brave enough—the French; but that is not the point. They are not good water fighters. By nature they are too hysterical, too easily excited, to both sail and fight a ship. Those English whom we go to meet are born water dogs, stubborn and cool; and the only ones afloat who, man for man, may match them are Americans."

"And of Americans you have but fifty?"

"Only fifty." Then, with a heartfelt oath: "I would give my left hand to have back my old crew of the Ranger."

Captain Paul Jones begins pacing to and fro, his thoughts running regretfully on the Ranger, and those stout hearts with whom he fought the Drake. But the Ranger and those stout, tarry ones are half a world away; and in the end he returns perforce to the Richard, and what poor tools in the way of crew are offered him by Fate. There is, too, a matter of gravity which he desires to lay before the Doctor's older and more prudent judgment. For Captain Paul Jones, so unmanageable by others, defers to the sagacious Doctor, and accepts his opinions and follows his commands with closed eyes.

"This Captain Pierre Landais, Doctor," he begins, "who is to sail the Alliance in my company?"

"Yes?" interrupts the Doctor.

"You know him?—you have confidence in him?"

The Doctor purses his lips, but says never a word.

"Then I'll tell you what I think!" cries Captain Paul Jones, who reads distrust in the good Doctor's pursed but silent lips; "I'll tell you what I think, and what I'll do. Already I've had some dealings with this Landais. The fellow is mad—vanity-mad. Jealous, insubordinate, he has twice taken open occasion to disobey my orders. This I have stomached in silence—being on French shores. I now warn you that as soon as I find myself in blue water, at a first sign of rebellion against my authority, I'll clap the fellow in irons. By heaven! I'll string him to his own yard arm, sir; make a tassel of him for the winds to play with, if it be required to preserve a discipline which his example has already done much to break down."

Doctor Franklin meets this violent setting forth concerning the recalcitrant Landais with a negative gesture of unmistakable emphasis.

"You must do nothing of the kind, Paul!" he replies. "Captain Landais, as you say, is doubtless mad—vanity-mad. But he is also French; and we must do nothing to estrange from our cause French sympathy and French assistance. I urge you to bear with Landais in silence, rather than jeopardize us with King Louis."

Captain Paul Jones growlingly submits. "It will result disastrously, Doctor," he says. "We shall yet suffer for it, mark my word." Then, disgustedly: "I marvel that the Marine Committee in Philadelphia should turn over to such a madman a brisk frigate like the Alliance.

"Your friend, the Marquis de Lafayette, had something to do with it, I think. You observe that on his present visit to France, it is Landais with his Alliance who brings him."

Captain Paul Jones says no more, but seems to accept Landais as he accepts the Richard, desperately. His final comment shows the uneasy complexion of his thought.

"We shall do the best we can, Doctor," he says.

"Young as I am, I have lived long enough to know that one can't have all things ordered as he would."

Captain Paul Jones, now commodore, clears for the Irish coast on a bright, clear day in June. Besides the Richard, he has with him the Alliance, thirty-two guns, Captain Landais; the Pallas, twenty-eight guns, Captain Cottineau; and the Vengeance, twelve guns, Captain Ricon. Four days later he returns limping into l'Orient for repairs, the Richard having been fouled by the Alliance through the criminal carelessness or worse of Captain Landais.

The breast of the young commodore is on fire with anger over the delay, and the vicious clumsiness that caused it. He burns to destroy Landais, as the mean reason of his troubles, but the thought of Doctor Franklin restrains him. Also, as events unfold, that enforced return to l'Orient proves of good fortune, and he forgets his chagrin in joy over the flattering new turn in his affairs. Doctor Franklin has succeeded in bringing about an exchange of prisoners, and barters to the British admiralty one hundred and nineteen Englishmen, captured in the Drake and other prizes taken by the Ranger, for one hundred and nineteen Americans held by King George. While Commodore Paul Jones is curing the damage done the Richard by the evil Landais, those exchanged Americans are landed under a cartel in Nantes. He goes down to Nantes and enlists one hundred and fifteen of them for the Richard.

Before Commodore Paul Jones weighs anchor for a second start, he goes over to Passy for a final word with Doctor Franklin. The pair walk in the Doctor's favorite garden, now a wilderness of foliage and flowers, the Doctor serene, the boy commodore cloudy, taciturn and grim. His resolution has set iron-hard to do or die; the cruise shall be a glorious one or be his last. Doctor Franklin asks about his plans.

"I shall make for the west coast of Ireland," says he, "and go north about the British islands. Wind and weather favoring, I may sack a town or two by way of retaliation for what the foe has done to us. They will find that I have not forgotten Lord Dunmore, and my ruined plantation by the Rappahannock."

"The waters you will sail in are alive with British ships of war. With your poor force it seems a desperate cruise."

"Desperate, yes; but, Doctor, we are in no shape to play cautious. We are weak; therefore we must be reckless."

"It is a strange doctrine," muses the Doctor. "And yet I will not say but what it smells of judgment. I have faith in you, Paul; it teaches me to hope that, when next I greet you, I shall greet a victor."

"Doctor," returns Commodore Paul Jones, and his tones are grave with meaning, "I shall not disappoint you. Nor do I care to conceal from you my resolution. When I sail, I sail looking for battle; and I shall not hesitate to engage an enemy superior to my force. The condition of our cause is such that, to sustain it, we need a striking, ay! a startling naval success, and I shall do all I know, fight all I know, to bring it to pass. More; my mind is made up: If I fail, I fall; I shall return victorious or I shall not return."

It is daybreak on a day in middle August when Commodore Paul Jones, with the Richard as flagship of the little squadron of four, puts the Isle of Groaix astern, and points for the open ocean. His course is west by north, so as to weather Cape Clear, and fetch the Irish coast close aboard. With winds light and baffling, the squadron's pace is slow; it is nine days out of France before Cape Clear is sighted. Then it creeps northward along the Irish coast, Commodore Paul Jones vigilant and alert. He takes a prize or two, and one after the other sends into French ports the British ships Mayflower and Fortune. The young commodore's brow begins to clear; those prizes comfort him vastly. At least the cruise shall not be registered as altogether fruitless.

It is the last day of August; the Hebrides lie off the Richard's starboard beam. A stiff gale from the northwest sets in, and the squadron is driven east by north under storm staysails. This dovetails with the desires of Commodore Paul Jones; wherefore he welcomes the gale as friendly weather. Also, it gives him a chance to try out the Richard, which shows lively with the wind abaft the beam, but dull to the confines of despair when sailing on a wind. Close-hauled, the Richard makes more lee than headway.

"Which means, Dick," says Commodore Paul Jones judgmatically, to Lieutenant Richard Dale—"which means, Dick, that we must have the weather-gage before we lock horns with an enemy."

Off Cape Wraith, Commodore Paul Jones is so fortunate as to take two further prizes. He turns them over to Captain Landais, with orders to send them into Brest. The Frenchman, who only receives an order for the purpose of breaking it, sends them into the port of Bergen, where the Norwegians promptly turn them over to the English, on an argument that they do not officially know of any government called the United States.

Commodore Paul Jones works slowly and cautiously southward along the east coast of Scotland. Off the Firth of Forth he decides to attack the Port of Leith, and stands in for that fell purpose. An adverse gale, seconded by off-shore currents, comes to the rescue of the threatened Scotchmen; in the teeth of his best seamanship Commodore Paul Jones and his squadron are driven out to sea. Thus the chance passes, and the sack of Leith is abandoned. It is a sore setback to the hopes of Commodore Paul Jones; but it lifts a load from the Scottish heart, to whom the Stars and Stripes have brought visions of pillage and torch and desolation. The news flies over England; beacons burn on each headland; while every semaphore is telling that the dreaded Paul Jones is hawking at the English coasts. The word causes a tremendous loss of British sleep.

Off Spurn Head our industrious young commodore sinks one collier and chases another ashore. Being full of curiosity, he takes a peep into the mouth of the Humber, and discovers a frightened fleet of British merchant vessels. The merchantmen are in a flutter at the sight of the Richard's dread topsails; the frigate that it conveying them has its work cut out, to nurse them into anything like calmness.

Following the look into the Humber, that sets so many timid merchantmen to shivering, Commodore Paul Jones puts out to sea under doublereefs. He plans to stand off and on throughout the night, and swoop on those tremblers, like a hawk on a covey of quail, with the first gray streaks of dawn. The frigate will doubtless fight, but the optimistic young commodore reckons on making short work of that man-of-war. In the middle watch the little brig Vengeance runs under the Richard's lee, bringing word of a nobler quarry. The Baltic timber fleet, fifty sail in all, convoyed by the Serapis and the Countess of Scarboro has just put into Bridlington Bay.

At this good news, Commodore Paul Jones gives up his designs touching the frightened covey of merchantmen in the Humber. He prefers the Baltic timber ships with the Serapis, the difference between the one and the other being the difference between deer and hare. He orders the Vengeance to stand out to sea, find the Alliance, and tell Captain Landais to join him off Scarboro' Head.

"But do not," says he to Captain Ricon, "give Captain Landais this notice in the guise of an order. He would make a point of disobeying, and seize on its reception as a pat occasion for insulting you."

While the Vengeance stands eastward in search of the Alliance, Commodore Paul Jones signals the __Pallas__ to follow, and turns his bows for Scarboro' Head, then forty miles away.

The Richard, the little Pallas close to its heels, cracks on canvas throughout the night. The winds are mere puffs and catspaws; still, slow as is their speed, daylight finds them within throwing distance of their destination. They are the wrong-side of the weather, however, and the whole day is wasted in beating inshore against the wind. Our young commodore must do all the work; for the English merchantmen, as though faint with fear at the sight of him, refuse to come out; while the Serapis and its consort stick close to them in their role of guardships. The sun goes down, night descends, and as yet our young commodore has not been able to get within reach of the foe; for at beating to windward the Richard is as dull as a Dutchman.

When darkness comes, it unlooses a land breeze. With that the merchantmen take heart of grace, and resolve to dare all and run for it. They rush out of Bridlington Bay, wind free, like a flock of seagulls. What is a fair wind for them is a headwind for the Richard and Pallas; with no one to molest them, the fifty timber ships show a clean pair of heels. Commodore Paul Jones makes no effort to chase; it would be seamanship thrown away. Besides, the Serapis has laid its sails aback, and is waiting to hear from him; while the Countess of Scarboro guarding the flanks of the fugitive timber ships, seems eagerly willing to try conclusions with the Pallas.

The temptation is too great; Commodore Paul Jones makes no least effort to resist it. Signaling the Pallas to close with and pull down the smaller ship, with his own eye on the Serapis, he begins manoeuvring for the upper hand. The sea is as smooth as glass; a great harvest moon shoots up in the cloudless sky. As when the Ranger fought the Drake, it is to be a fight by the light of the moon.

The Richard tacks starboard and port, the Serapis lying in wait. Decks cleared, guns shotted and run out, magazines open, men stripped and at their quarters, both ships are as ferociously ready as bulldogs. Commodore Paul Jones scans the Serapis through his glass.

"How heavy is he, Commodore?"

It is Dr. Brooke, surgeon of the Richard, who puts the question. He has been laying out his instruments and bandages in the cockpit, in readiness for a hard night's work, and now pokes his nose on deck for a last breath of fresh air.

"Is that you, Doctor?" returns Commodore Paul Jones. The amiable tones bespeak that bland urbanity which is his dominant characteristic on the threshold of battle. "It's the Serapis; a forty-four-gun ship of the Rainbow class, six months off the stocks."

It should be observed that Commodore Paul Jones' pet study is the British navy, and he knows more about it—ships, guns, and men—than does the king's admiralty itself.

"Forty-four guns! Rainbow class!" repeats the worthy doctor, who himself is not without a working knowledge of ships and their comparative strengths. "Then she's a stronger ship, with heavier metal, than the Richard?"

"As three is to two, Doctor," replies Commodore Paul Jones, shutting up his glass and preparing for action. "None the less, we shall fight them and beat them just the same."

Aboard the Serapis, Captain Pearson is holding his glass on the Richard, not a cable's length away. Suddenly the Richard wears and backs its topsail, thereby bringing its broadside to bear upon the Serapis.

"That was a clever manoeuvre!" remarks Captain Pearson, admiringly, to Lieutenant Wright, who stands by his side. "It holds for him the weather-gage, and makes it impossible for me to luff across his hawse, without exposing my ship to be raked."

"Who is he?" asks Lieutenant Wright; for the Serapis is just home from Norway, and the word that set all England to lighting beacons and doubling coast-guards has not reached it.

"Who is he?" repeats Captain Pearson, soberly. "He is Paul Jones; and, my word for it, Lieutenant, there is work ahead."

CHAPTER XV
THE "RICHARD" AND THE "SERAPIS"

The ships are slowly closing, watchful as wrestlers striving for holds, the Richard edging down with the wind, the Serapis holding on.

"What ship is that?" hails Captain Pearson.

There is no reply.

"What ship is that?" comes the second hail.

The response is a storm of solid shot from the Richard's flaming broadside.

As the Richard goes into action, Commodore Paul Jones swings his glass along the eastern horizon. The Pallas is going down the wind, in hot pursuit of the Countess of Scarboro, yawing and firing its bow-chaser as it runs; while far out to sea lies the traitor Landais, sulking or skulking, it matters little which, his coward topsails just visible against the moonlit sky-line.

With the wind aft, the Richard and the Serapis head northwest, both on the port tack. The moon makes the scene as light as day; the sea is as evenly smooth as a ballroom floor. The Richard goes over on the starboard tack, the Serapis holding as she is; the ships approach each other, the Richard keeping the weather-gage. For twenty minutes it is broadside and broadside as fast as men may handle sponge and rammer. As in the hour of the Drake and Ranger, the Yankees show smarter with their guns.

When the battle begins, the Richard has to its broadside three eighteen-pounders, as against the Serapis' ten. With the first fire, two of the Richard's three explode, killing half the men that serve them, and tearing open the main gun-deck immediately above. Lieutenant Mayrant, who has command in the gunroom where the three eighteens are mounted, reports the disaster to Commodore Paul Jones. The latter receives the news beamingly, as though it were the enemies' eighteen-pounders, and not his own, that have been put out of action.

"Then we have only the twelve-pounders and the long nines to fight him with," says Commodore Paul Jones. "It is now a thirty-two-gun ship against a forty-four. We shall beat him; and the honor will be the greater." Then, observing Lieutenant Mayrant to be severely wounded in the head, he becomes concerned for that young gentleman. "Better go below to Brooks," says he, "and have your wounds dressed."

"I must get square for Portsea jail first," replies Lieutenant Mayrant, who is of those exchanged ones enlisted at Nantes.

Lieutenant Dale, forward with the twelve-pounders, comes aft to ask about the exploded eight guns.

"They were rotten when the Frenchmen sold them to us," says Lieutenant Dale bitterly.

"Ay!" responds Commodore Paul Jones. "I'd give half the prize money I shall get from yonder ship to have those Frenchmen here." Meanwhile the Serapis—not yet a prize—is fiercely belching flame and smoke, while her shot tear the vitals out of the Richard.

The ships have been fighting half an hour—rough broadside work; the Richard with its lighter metal has had the worst of the barter. They have sailed, or rather drifted, a mile and a half, edging closer to one another as they forge slowly to the north and west.

The Serapis, being the livelier ship, has fore-reached on the Richard, and Captain Pearson sees the chance to luff across the latter's bows. Having torn the Richard open with a raking broadside, Captain Pearson will then go clear around the Yankee, put the Serapis upon the starboard tack, and claim in his turn the weather-gage. It is a brilliant thought, and Captain Pearson pulls down his helm to execute it. Already he sees victory in his fingers. He is radiant; it will make him a Knight Commander of the Bath.

While Captain Pearson is manoeuvring for that title, the hot broadside dispute proceeds with unflagging fury. Only the Richard is beginning to bleed and gasp; those ten eighteen-pounders of the Serapis overmaster its weaker batteries. Also, by this time they are doubly weak; for more than half of the Richard's twelve-pounders have been dismounted, and the balance are so jammed with wreckage and splinters as to forbid them being worked. Lieutenant Dale reports the crippled condition of the Richard's broadside to Commodore Paul Jones, where the latter stands on the after-deck, in personal command of the French marines, whose captain has crept below with a hurt knee.

"We have but three effective twelve-pounders left," says Lieutenant Dale.

"Three?" retorts Commodore Paul Jones, cheerfully. "Now, well-aimed and low, Dick, much good damage may be worked with three twelve-pounders."

Lieutenant Dale wipes the blood and sweat and powder-stains from his face, salutes, and goes back to his three guns; while Commodore Paul Jones, alive to the enemy's new manouvre, takes the wheel from the quartermaster.

To check the ambitious Pearson in his efforts to luff across his forefoot, Commodore Paul Jones pays off the Richard's head a point. The check is not alone successful, but under the influence of that master hand, the Richard all but gets the Serapis' head into chancery.

Being defeated in his luff, Captain Pearson next discovers that his brisk antagonist has put him in a dilemma. If he holds on, the Richard will run him down; he can already see the great, black cutwater rearing itself on high, as though to crush him and cut him in two. If he pays off the head of the Serapis, and avoids being run down, the Richard will still foul and grapple with him. Lieutenant Mayrant's bandaged head shows above the Richard's hammock nettings, as, with grappling irons ready for throwing, he musters a party of boarders—cutlass and pistol and pike—to have them in hand the moment the ships crash together. That title of Knight Commander of the Bath, and the star and garter that go with it, do not look so near at hand. Also, the Serapis, at this closer range, begins to feel the musket-fire from the Richard's tops. One after another, three seamen are shot down at the wheel of the Serapis.

In this desperate emergency, Captain Pearson, good sailorman that he is, neither holds on nor pays off, but with everything thrown aback attempts to box-haul his ship. It may take the sticks out by the roots, but he must risk it. The chance is preferable to being either run down or boarded.

The Serapis is a new ship, fresh from the yards, and her spars and cordage stand the strain. Captain Pearson backs himself slowly out of the trap. He grazes fate so closely that the Richard, answering some sudden occult movement of the helm, runs its bowsprit over the larboard quarter of the Serapis, into its mizzen rigging.

"Stand by with those grappling irons!" shouts Commodore Paul Jones.

Lieutenant Mayrant throws the grapples with a seaman's accuracy; they catch, as he means they shall, in the mizzen backstays of the Englishman. But the ships have too much way on. The Richard forges ahead; the Serapis, every sail flattened, backs free; the lines part. Before Lieutenant Mayrant can take his jolly boarders over the Richard's bows, the ships have swung apart, and fifty feet of open water yawn between them.

The Serapis falls to leeward; at the end of the next five minutes both ships are back in their old positions, with their broadside guns—or what are left of them—at that furious work of hammer and tongs.

At this crashing business of broadsiding, the Richard has no chance, and Commodore Paul Jones—a smile on his dauntless lips, eyes bright and glancing like those of a child with a new toy—stands well aware of it. He must board the Englishman, or he is lost. As showing what Captain

Pearson's eighteen-pounders can do, the Richard's starboard battery—being the one in action—shows nine of its twelve-pounders dismounted from their carriages; while, of the one hundred and forty-three officers and men who belong with the main gun-deck battery under Lieutenant Dale, eighty-seven lie dead and wounded. The gun-deck itself, a-litter with dismounted guns and shot-smashed carriages and tackle, is slippery with blood, and choked by a red clutter of dead and wounded sailors.

Commodore Paul Jones turns to his orderly,

Jack Downes. "Present my compliments to Lieutenant Dale," says lie, "and ask him to step aft."

Bloody, powder-grimed, Lieutenant Dale responds.

"Dick," observes Commodore Paul Jones, "he's too heavy for us. We must close with him; we must get hold of him. Bring what men you have to the spar-deck, and serve out the small arms for boarding."

The breeze veers to the west, and freshens up a bit. This helps the Richard sooner than it does the Serapis; Commodore Paul Jones, having advantage of it, wears and makes directly for his enemy. This move, like a stroke of genius, brings him within one hundred feet of the Serapis, directly between it and the wind. It is his purpose to blanket the enemy, and steal the breeze from him. He succeeds; the Serapis loses way.

It is now the turn of Commodore Paul Jones to go across his enemy's forefoot, and retort upon the Serapis that manouvre which Captain Pearson attempted against the Richard. But with this difference: Captain Pearson's purpose was to rake; Commodore Paul Jones' purpose is to board; for he lias now no guns wherewith to rake.

The Serapis is held as though in irons, canvas a-flap, by the blanket of the Richard's broad sails. Slowly yet surely, like the coming of a doom, the Richard forges across the other's head. The design of Commodore Paul Jones is to lay the Serapis aboard, lash ship to ship, and sweep the Englishman's decks with his boarders. These, armed to the teeth, as ready for the rush as so many hunting dogs, Lieutenant Mayrant is holding in the waist.

The Richard is half its length across the bows of the Serapis—still helpless, sails a-droop! Suddenly, by a twist of the helm, Commodore Paul Jones broaches the Richard to on the opposite tack, and doubles down on his prey. It is the beginning of the end. The jib-boom of the Serapis runs in over the poop-deck of the Richard; a turn is instantly taken on it with a small hawser by Lieutenant Dale, who makes all fast to the Richard's mizzen-mast. The ships swing closer and closer together; at last the two rasp broadside against broadside, the Richard still holding its way. As they grind along, the outboard fluke of the Serapis' starboard anchor catches in the Richard's mizzen-chains. First one, then another gives way; the third holds, and the ships lie together bow and stern. Commodore Paul Jones is over the side like a cat; the next moment he lashes the Serapis to the Richard, and the death-hug is at hand.

CHAPTER XVI
HOW THE BATTLE RAGED

Commodore Paul Jones drops overboard his cocked hat. Orderly Jack Downes rushes into the cabin and gets another. Returning, he offers it to Commodore Paul Jones, who waves it away with a laugh.

"Chuck it through the skylight, Jack," he says; "I'll fight this out in my scalp." Then, glancing forward at the sailors, naked to the waist: "If it were not for the looks of the thing, I'd off coat and shirt, and fight in the buff like yonder gallant hearties."

There is a sudden smashing of the Richard's bulwarks, a splintering of spars; a sleet of shot, grape and solid and bar, tears through the ship! In the wake of that hail of iron comes the thunder of the guns—loud and close aboard! Commodore Paul Jones looks about in angry wonder; that broadside was not from the Serapis!

"It's the Alliance!" cries Lieutenant Dale, rushing aft. "Landais is firing on us!"

Not half a cable-length away lies the Alliance, head to the wind, topsails back, half hidden in a curling smother of powder-smoke. There comes but the one broadside. Even as Commodore Paul Jones looks, the traitor's head pays slowly off; a moment later the sails belly and fill, and the Alliance is running seaward before the wind. Commodore Paul Jones grits out a curse.

"Landais! Was ever another such a villain out of hell!"

The villain Landais makes off. There is no time for maledictions; besides, a court-martial will come later for that miscreant. Just now Captain Pearson, with his Serapis, claims the attention of Commodore Paul Jones.

The tackle takes the strain; the lashings, and that fortunate starboard anchor of the Serapis, hold the ships together. Captain Pearson sees the peril, and the way to free himself.

"Cut away that sta'board anchor!" he cries. Then, as a seaman armed with a hatchet springs forward, he continues: "The ring-stopper, man! Cut the shank-painter and the ring-stopper; let the anchor go!"

Commodore Paul Jones snatches a firelock from one of the agitated French marines. Steadying himself against a backstay, he raises the weapon to his shoulder and fires. The ball goes crashing through the seaman's head as he raises his hatchet to cut free the anchor. Another leaps forward and grasps the hatchet. Seizing a second firelock, Commodore Paul Jones stretches him across the anchor's shank, where he lies clutching and groaning and bleeding his life away. As the second man goes down, those nearest fall back. That fatal starboard anchor is a death-trap; they want none of it! Commodore Paul Jones, alert as a wildcat and as bent for blood, keeps grim watch, firelock in fist, at the backstay.

"I turned those hitches with my own hands," says he; "and I'll shoot down any Englishman who meddles with them."

The French marines, despite the hardy example of Commodore Paul Jones, are in a panic. Their Captain Cammillard is wounded, and has retired below. Now their two lieutenants are gone. Besides, of the more than one hundred to go into the fight, no more than twenty-five remain. These, nerve-shattered and deeming all as lost, are fallen into disorder and dismay. The centuries have taught them to fear these sullen English. The lesson has come down to them in the blood of their fathers who fought at Crécy, Poitiers, Blenheim, Ramillies, and Malplaquet that these bulldog islanders are unconquerable! Panic grasps them at the moment of all moments when Commodore Paul Jones requires them most.

Seeing them thus shaken and beaten in their hearts, Commodore Paul Jones—who knows Frenchmen in their impulses as he knows his own face in a glass—adopts the theatrical. He rushes into their midst, thundering:

"Courage, my friends! What a day for France is this! We have these dogs of English at our mercy! Courage but a little while, my friends, and the day is ours! Oh, what a day for France!" As adding éclat to that day for France, Commodore Paul Jones snatches a third firelock from the nearest marine, and shoots down a third Briton who, hatchet upraised, is rushing upon that detaining anchor. Following this exploit, he wheels again upon those wavering marines, and by way of raising their spirits pours forth in French such a cataract of curses upon all Englishmen and English things that it fairly exhausts the imagination of his hearers to keep abreast of it.

Pierre Gerard, the little Breton sailor who, with Jack Downes, acts as orderly to Commodore Paul Jones, is swept off his feet in admiration of his young commander's fire and profane fluency. Little Pierre takes fire in his turn.

"See!" he cries, addressing Jack Downes, who being from New Hampshire understands never a word of Pierre's French, albeit he takes it in, open-mouthed, like spring water; "See! He springs among them like a tiger among calves! Ah, they respond to him! Yes, in an instant he arouses their courage! They look upon him—him, who has bravery without end! Name of God! To see him is to become a hero!"

It is as the excitable little Pierre recounts. The French marines, lately so cowed, look upon Commodore Paul Jones to become heroes. With shouts and cries they crowd about him valorously. He directs their fire against the English, who man the long-nines in the open waist of the Serapis. The fire of the recovered Frenchmen drives those English from their guns. Thereupon the French go wild with a fierce joy, and are all for boarding the Serapis. Commodore Paul Jones has as much trouble restraining them from rushing forward as he had but a moment before to keep them from falling back.

Captain Pearson has never taken his eyes from that fatal starboard anchor, holding him fast to the Richard. There it lies, his own anchor—the keystone to the arch of his ruin! If it take every English life aboard the Serapis, it must be cut away! He orders four men forward in a body, to cut shank-painter and ring-stopper.

There comes an instant volley from the recovered French marines, led by Commodore Paul Jones, who fires with them. Before that withering volley the four hatchet-men fall in a crumpled, bloody heap. The fatal anchor still holds; the ships grind side by side.

Captain Pearson orders forward more men, and still more men, to cut away that anchor, which is as an anchor of death, tying him broadside and broadside to destruction. Fourteen men die, one across the other, under the fire of Commodore Paul Jones and his French marines—each of the latter being now a volcano of fiery valor! The last to perish is Lieutenant Popplewill; he dies honorably at the hands of Commodore Paul Jones himself, who sends a musket ball through the high heart of the young dreadnought just as he reaches those fatal fastenings.

While this labor of death and bloody slaughter goes on above, the smashing work of the Serapis' eighteen-pounders has not ceased between decks. As the two ships come together, the lower-tier gun crews of the Serapis are shifted from the port to the starboard batteries. They attempt to run out the guns, and are withstood by the port-lids, which refuse to be triced up, the Richard grinding them so hard and close as to hold them fast.

"What!" cries Lieutenant Wright, who has command of the Serapis' eighteen-pounders; "the ports won't open? Open them with your round-shot, then, my hearties! Fire!"

And so the broadside of the Serapis is fired through its own planks and timbers, to open a way to the Richard.

"There!" cries Lieutenant Wright exultantly, "that should give your guns a chance to breathe, my bucks! Now show us how fast you can send your iron aboard the Yankee!"

The English broadside men respond with such goodwill that they literally cut the Richard in two between decks with their tempest of solid eighteen-pound shot.

While this smashing battery work goes forward, hammer and anvil, the Serapis' twelve-pounders are tearing and rending the Richard's upper decks, piling them in ruins. Every twelve-pounder belonging to the Richard is rendered dumb. Only three long-nines remain in service. These are mounted on the quarter-deck, under the eye of Commodore Paul Jones.

"Suppose, Mr. Lindthwait, you train them on the enemy's mainmast!" he observes to the midshipman, under whose command he places the three long-nines. "Try for his mainmast, young man! It will be good gunnery practise for you; and should you cut the stick in two, so much the better."

Midshipman Lindthwait serves his trio of long nines with so much relish and vivacious accuracy that he soon has the mainmast of the Serapis cut half away. Leaving him to his task, Commodore Paul Jones again takes his French marines in hand, uplifts their souls with a fresh torrent of anti-English vituperation, and keeps them to the business of clearing the enemy's deck.

One of the nine-pound shot of the industrious Lindthwait, flying low, strikes the main hatch of the Serapis, and slews the hatch cover to one side. It leaves a triangular opening, eighteen inches on its longish side, at one corner of the hatch. Commodore Paul Jones has his hawklike eye on it instantly. He points it out to midshipman Fanning and gunner Henry Gardner.

"There's your chance, my lads!" he cries. "Sharp's the word now! Lay aloft on the main topsail yard, with a bucketful of hand-grenades, and see if you can't chuck one into her belly. A few hand-grenades, exploding among their eighteen-pounders below decks, would go far towards showing these English the error of their ways."

Off skurry Midshipman Fanning and Gunner Gardner, with three sailors close behind. A moment later they are racing up the shrouds like monkeys, two ratlins at a time. Buckets of hand-grenades go with them, while Lieutenant Stack rigs a whip to the maintop to send them up a fresh supply.

The five lie out on the main topsail yard, like a quintette of squirrels, midshipman Fanning, a bright lad from New London, getting the place of honor at the earring. The three sailors pass the hand-grenades, gunner Gardner fires the fuse with his slow match, while midshipman Fanning, perched at the farthest end of the yard, hurls them at that eighteen-inch triangle, where the hatch cover of the Serapis has been shifted.

Sixty feet below the hand-grenade quintette, Commodore Paul Jones is again dealing out profane encouragement to his marines, for their ardor sensibly slackens the moment he takes his eye off them. They do good work, however—these Frenchmen! Under their fire the upper deck of the Serapis becomes a slaughter-pen. One after another, seven men are shot down at the Englishman's wheel. This does not affect the Serapis; since, locked together in the death grapple, both ships are adrift, and have paid no attention to their helms for twenty minutes. Still, it does the Frenchmen good to shoot down those wheelmen. Also, it mortifies the pride of the English; for to be unable to stay at one's own wheel is in its way a disgrace.

While Commodore Paul Jones is uplifting his Frenchmen, and improving their small-arm practice, orderly Jack Downes, who has been forward to Lieutenant Dale with an order, comes rushing aft.

"Lieutenant Dale, sir, reports six feet of water in our hold; and coming in fast, sir!"

Orderly Jack Downes touches his forelock, face as stolid aw a statue's, and not at all as though he has just reported the ship to be sinking. Commodore Paul Jones smiles approval on stolid Jack Downes; he likes coolness and self-command. Before he can speak, Lieutenant Mayrant comes aft to say that the Richard is on fire.

"Catches from the enemy's wadding," says Lieutenant Mayrant. "For you must understand, sir, that when the enemy's eighteen-pounders are run out, their muzzles pierce through the shot-holes in our sides—we lay that close! As it is, they've set us all ablaze."

"But you've got the flames in hand?" Commodore Paul Jones puts the question confidently. He is sure that Lieutenant Mayrant wouldn't be by his side at that moment unless the fire is under command.

"Lieutenant Stack, with ten men to pass the buckets, sir, are attending to it. It's quite easy, the water in our hold being so deep. They have but to dip it up and throw it on the fire."

"Good!" exclaimed Commodore Paul Jones. "Now that's what I call making one hand wash the other. We put out the flames that are eating us up with the water that is sinking us."

CHAPTER XVII
THE SURRENDER OF THE "SERAPIS"

Master-at-arms John Burbank looks over the Richard's side, and makes a discovery. The ship has settled three feet below its trim. Thereupon he loses his head, which was never a strong head, but somewhat thick, and addled:

"The ship is sinking!" he shouts; then, being a humanitarian, he tears off the orlop-hatch, and calls to the two hundred prisoners shut up below to save themselves.

At the invitation of Humanitarian Burbank, the prisoners rush up. Fifty of them have gained the deck when Commodore Paul Jones perceives them. Pulling a pistol from his belt, he charges forward.

"Who released these prisoners?" he demands.

"The ship is sinking, sir," replies Humanitarian Burbank. "I released them to give them a chance for their lives."

Eye ablaze, Commodore Paul Jones snaps his pistol in the face of Humanitarian Burbank. Fortunately for that philanthropist, the priming has been shaken out; while the flint throws off a shower of sparks, the pistol does not explode. Upon its failure to fire. Commodore Paul Jones clubs the heavy weapon, and fells Humanitarian Burbank to the deck. The latter comes to presently, to find himself disrated on the ship's books, and his addled pate more addled than before. As Humanitarian Burbank falls to the deck, Commodore Paul Jones makes a dash for the prisoners, who, two abreast, are pushing up from the deck below.

"Under hatches with them!" he cries.

This rouses Midshipman Potter, who brings up a half dozen cutlass men, and those of the prisoners not yet on deck are held below. The orlop-hatch is again fitted to its place, and Commodore Paul Jones breathes freer. Two hundred prisoners loose about his decks is not what he most desires.

"Set them to the pumps, Dick," he says, addressing Lieutenant Dale. "Give them plenty of work." Then, to the fifty prisoners who gained the deck: "Now, my men, to the pumps, all of you! I'll have no idlers about!"

The prisoners go to the pumps readily enough—all save a stubborn merchant captain, whose ship was captured by the Richard off the port of Leith.

"Don't ye go a-nigh the pumps, mates!" sings out the stubborn one. "Let the damned Yankee pirate sink!"

"Obey the Commodore, sare!" pipes up little Pierre Gerard, presenting a pistol at the head of the mutineer. "Obey the Commodore, or I shoot, sare!"

The stubborn Scotch captain does not understand little Pierre's broken English, but the pistol is easily construed. For reply, he makes a quick grab at the weapon. Little Pierre, not to be caught napping, shoots him promptly through the head. As the stubborn one drops lifeless, the little Breton wheels on Commodore Paul Jones, lays his hand on his heart, and makes an apologetic bow.

"I shoot heem, sare, to relieve you of a disagreeable duty," says little Pierre.

The other prisoners are not unimpressed by the fate of the stubborn one, and set to work briskly, if not cheerfully, at the clanking pumps.

As Commodore Paul Jones reaches the quarterdeck, following the incident wherein Humanitarian Burbank performs, and the stubborn Scotch captain dies, the ensign-gaff of the Richard is shot away, and the virgin petticoat flag of the pretty New Hampshire girls trails overboard. This gives rise to a misunderstanding. Gunner Arthur Randall, missing the ensign, and his hopes being somewhat low at the time, calls out to the Englishman:

"Cease firing! We've surrendered!"

Captain Pearson, on the quarter-deck of the Serapis, hears the cry. There could have come no more welcome news! Captain Pearson would have heard gunner Randall if the latter had spoken in a whisper! Face aglow with joy, Captain Pearson hails the Richard:

"Do you surrender?" he demands.

Commodore Paul Jones leaps to the rail of the Richard, and sustains himself by one of the afterbraces.

"Surrender?" he repeats, his brow dark with rage. "Surrender? I would have you to know, sir, that we've just begun to fight!"

Back to the deck springs Commodore Paul Jones, while the face of Captain Pearson is stricken old and white. For the earliest time he realizes the desperate heart of that unconquerable one who has him in a death-grapple, and a premonition of his own defeat pierces his heart like a dagger of ice. As Commodore Paul Jones regains the deck, he observes Boatswain Jack Robinson who has waddled aft. The cloud of anger fades from his brow, and he breaks into a loud laugh that is tenfold worse than the cloud.

"Eh, Jack, old trump! What say you to quitting?" he cries.

"Why! as to surrenderin', Commodore," says Boatswain Jack Robinson, refreshing himself with a huge chew of tobacco, "I'm for sinkin' alongside an' seein' 'em damned first! Sink alongside, says I; an' if the grapplin' tackle holds, we'll take 'em with us to Davy Jones, d'ye see! An' that'll be a comfort!"

"There's the heart of oak!" returns Commodore Paul Jones, in vast approval of Boatswain Jack Robinson's turgid views; "and when we're next ashore in New London, old shipmate, I'll tell Polly all about it. Meanwhile, our ensign's trailing astern. Set it aboard by the halyards, fish and splice the gaff, and put it back in its place. Give the Englishmen a sight of that red, white and blue flag, Jack; it takes the fight out of 'em."

"Ay, ay, sir!" responds Boatswain Jack Robinson, as he begins the task of recovering and replacing the ensign. "That flag does seem to let the whey out of a Britisher."

This is gratuitous slander on the parts of both Commodore Paul Jones and Boatswain Jack Robinson; for those villified ones have been fighting for hours, and are still at it with the quenchless valor of so many mastiffs.

There is that at hand, however, that will daunt their iron courage and feed even their stout hearts to dismay. High up at the weather earring of the Richard's main topsail yard, Midshipman Fanning has been faithfully practicing with hand-grenades at that inviting triangular hole, where the hatch-cover of the Serapis was shot-slewed to one side. It is not an easy mark, that black, three-cornered hole, and thus far Midshipman Fanning has missed. It is now that success crowns his work; a smoking, spitting hand-grenade goes cleanly through, and fetches up on the Serapis's lower gun deck. The explosion instantly occurs; it is as though the fuse were carefully timed for it.

If this were all it would be bad enough, but worse comes with it. There are scores of cartridges cumbering the deck to the rear of the batteries; for the powder monkeys of the Serapis, earning their pay and allowances, have been bringing powder from the magazines much faster than the gunners can burn it in their eighteen-pounders. The exploding hand-grenade sets off this powder. There is a blinding sheet of flame; a report like smothered thunder; the deck of the Serapis is all but torn from its timbers! Fifty of the crew are killed or crippled, while the slewed hatch-cover is blown overboard. No trouble now to hit that yawning black hatchway. With such a target there can be no talk of missing, and Midshipman Fanning and gunner Gardner, from their high perch on the main topsail yard, fill the stomach of the Serapis with a bursting, death-dealing shower. And so the end comes tapping at the door.

Lieutenant Mayrant, with his boarding party, stands waiting the signal. Commodore Paul Jones notes the devastation wrought by Midshipman Fanning's hand-grenades.

"Boarders away!" he cries.

Lieutenant Mayrant and his men go swarming over the hammock nettings of the Serapis, the red Indian port-fire, Anthony Jeremiah, among the foremost.

As Lieutenant Mayrant reaches the deck of the Serapis, an English sailor thrusts him through the thigh with a pike. Lieutenant Mayrant shoots the pikeman though the heart. The latter falls dead, pike rattling along the deck.

"Remember Portsea jail, lads!" shouts Lieutenant Mayrant, as he strides limpingly across the body of the dead pikeman. "Remember Port-sea jail!"

Nine in ten of the boarding party are of those ones exchanged at Nantes. With savage cries, they shout back, "Remember Portsea jail!" and the work of their vengeance is begun.

Commodore Paul Jones has his eyes on Lieutenant Mayrant and his boarders. His attention is claimed by orderly Jack Downes, who plucks him by the elbow.

"Beg pardon, sir!" says orderly Jack Downes. "Captain Landais with the Alliance."

Sure enough, the Alliance for a second time has crept down upon them, unnoticed in the heat and absorbing fury of the fray. The consort ship is wearing across the Richard's bows. What will Landais do? Does he come as friend or foe? The Frenchman has his answer ready, and pours a broadside into the Richard as he crosses. Then he sheers off, and again heads for the open ocean. That coward broadside kills and wounds Master's Mate Caswell and seven men. Commodore Paul Jones is rigid with rage and wonder.

"The man is mad!" says Lieutenant Dale.

"I cannot understand!" returns Commodore Paul Jones. "There is still his crew! Why don't they clap him in irons, or cut him down?"

There is a shout from the deck of the Serapis. Captain Pearson, his last hope gone, has struck his colors with his own hand. The shout is from the wounded Lieutenant Mayrant, who hails Lieutenant Dale.

"Stop the firing, sir," cries Lieutenant May-rant, for the Richard's top-men are still blazing away merrily. "He has struck his flag. Come on board, and take possession!"

Lieutenant Dale leaps to the deck of the beaten Serapis. He sends Captain Pearson aboard the Richard. Downcast, eye full of dejection, Captain Pearson approaches Commodore Paul Jones. "With bowed head, saying never a word, he tenders the conqueror his sheathed sword. Commodore Paul Jones takes it and gives it to Midshipman Potter, who is at his elbow.

"I accept your sword, Captain," says Commodore Paul Jones. "And I bear testimony that you have worn it to the glory of the English navy."

Captain Pearson makes no response. Bowed of head, mute of lip, he stands before Commodore Paul Jones, despair eating his heart.

CHAPTER XVIII
DIPLOMACY AND THE DUTCH

Commodore Paul Jones goes aboard the beaten Serapis. "Cut free that sta'board anchor!" he cries. The piled dead and wounded are lifted aside, and that fatal anchor, which for two hours of blood has been as the backbone of battle, goes splashing into the ocean. The ships rock apart; as they separate, Commodore Paul Jones takes a sharp survey of the Richard. The survey brings little hope; his good ship that has fought so well for him lies in the water four smothering feet below its trim.

"There are eight feet of water in the hold," replies Lieutenant Dale, whom he hails. "The pumps choke; there's no chance to save the ship."

Then arises a sudden rending and tearing aboard the Serapis; there is a great swish! and a snapping of cordage. It is the mainmast crashing to port, a tangle of ropes and spars.

"Beg pardon, sir," says a voice at the elbow of Commodore Paul Jones. "I'd have had it down an hour ago, but there was neither wind nor swell to help me. I had to cut it in two shot by shot to drop it, sir."

Commodore Paul Jones breaks into a smile. "Ah, yes; I remember, Mr. Lindthwait! I set you at that mainmast with the three long nines. I wish now that I'd given you another target. However, you did extremely well. It should teach you, too, my lad, that a nine is as good as an eighteen, if you'll only go close enough. That's it; there's the whole secret of success in war. Be sure and go close enough, and you will conquer."

Midshipman Lindthwait salutes respectfully, and lays away that golden rule of the battle art in his memory.

The removal of the Richard's wounded is begun. The calm, windless sea assists; at last no one is left aboard the shot-pierced Richard but the dead.

Sixty lionhearts, who gave their lives for victory, are laid side by side on the deck. The petticoat flag flies proudly from the ensign gaff. Commodore Paul Jones, from the deck of the Serapis, watches the Richard to the last. The tears dim his sight, and he is driven more than once to dash them away; for a sailor loves his ship as though it were a woman.

The Richard settles by the head; the stern is lifted clear of the water. Then, as though seized by some impulse, the Richard, bows first, dives for the bottom of the sea. The last that is seen, as the stout old ship goes down, is the virgin petticoat flag of the pretty Portsmouth girls. Commodore Paul Jones, bare of head, tears blinding his eyes, waves a last farewell.

"Good-bye, my lads!" he cries. "And you, too, my Richard; good-bye!"

The Pallas comes up, breeze aft. The little ship throws its head into the wind, and Captain Cot-tineau hails Commodore Paul Jones.

"I have the honor, sir," says Captain Cottineau, "to report the enemy's surrender of his ship."

Captain Cottineau points with his speaking-trumpet to the Countess of Scarboro a furlong astern, the stars and stripes above the Union Jack.

Commodore Paul Jones congratulates Captain Cottineau, and tells him to make sail for Dunkirk with his prize. Captain Cottineau, observing the helpless Serapis, its deck a jungle of cordage and broken timbers, replies that if Commodore Paul Jones doesn't mind he'd sooner stand by. Commodore Paul Jones doesn't mind, and so Captain Cottineau, with the Pallas and the captured Scarboro stands by. The loyalty of Captain Cottineau flushes the bronzed cheek of Commodore Paul Jones. It is a change from the villain Landais! Ah, yes! Landais! The brow of Commodore Paul Jones turns black with anger; for a moment he forgot the scoundrel. He runs his glass along the horizon to seaward. There is no sign of the Alliance. Long ago the traitor Landais turned his recreant bows for France.

An off-shore gale springs up; adrift and helpless, the Serapis is carried seventy miles towards the coast of Norway. This is fortunate; it carries the ship outside the search of those twenty frigates and ships of the line, which are already furiously ransacking the English coast in quest of Commodore Paul Jones.

The wind veers to the southwest, and blows a hurricane. The Serapis is all but thrown upon the coast of Denmark, and has work to keep afloat. With one hundred and six wounded, and the dead who went down with the Richard, Commodore Paul Jones is short of hands to work his ship. At the best, no more than one hundred and fifty are fit for duty. In the end the battered Serapis makes the Texel, and a common sigh of relief goes up from those seven hundred and twelve souls—crew and wounded and prisoners—who are aboard the ship.

And now Commodore Paul Jones must lay aside his sword for chicane, abandon his guns in favor of diplomacy. His anchors are hardly down in Dutch mud, before Sir Joseph Yorke, English Ambassador to Holland, demands the Serapis from the Dutch authorities. Also, he declares that they must arrest Commodore Paul Jones "as a rebel and a pirate."

The Dutch display a wish to argue the case with Sir Joseph, while Commodore Paul Jones double-shots his guns and runs them out; for much in the way of repairs has been effected aboard the Serapis, and although it can't sail it can fight.

Sir Joseph, at the grinning insolence of the Serapis' broadsides—ports triced up and muzzles showing—almost falls in an apoplectic fit. Purple as to face, he sends a second time to the Dutch, to learn whether or no he is to have the Serapis and the rebel and pirate Paul Jones.

For five days the Dutch drink beer, smoke pipes, and think the matter over. Then they tell Sir Joseph that, while they don't know what to call Commodore Paul Jones, they have decided not to call him a pirate. Rebel, he may be; but in that role of rebel King George and Sir Joseph must catch him for themselves. The most the Dutch will do is order the Serapis to leave the Texel. At this the empurpled Sir Joseph becomes more empurpled than ever. It is the best he can get, however; and since, during the night, a fleet of British men of war, hearing of the whereabouts of Commodore Paul Jones, have invested the mouth of the Helder and are waiting for him to come out, he begins to be a trifle comforted. If the Dutch will but drive the "rebel" from the port, it should do nicely; the English fleet outside will snap him up at a mouthful.

Commodore Paul Jones refuses to be driven out. He sits stubbornly by his anchors, decks cleared, guns shotted, boarding nettings up—an insult to the purple Sir Joseph and a frowning defiance to the Dutch! The Dutch and Sir Joseph look at him, and then at each other. They agree that he is either the most exasperating of rebels, or the most insolent of pirates, or the most impertinent of guests, according to their various standpoints.

Meanwhile, the French Ambassador is bestirring himself. He makes a stealthy visit to Commodore Paul Jones. The French king has sent him, post-haste, a commission as Captain in the French marine. The French Ambassador tenders the commission. Upon accepting it, Commodore Paul Jones can run up the French flag. The Dutch will respect the tri-color, and there will come no more orders for the Serapis to quit the Texel.

Commodore Paul Jones declines the French commission. Neither will he run up the French flag. "I am an officer of the American Navy," says he, "and the French tri-color no more belongs at my masthead than at General Washington's headquarters. I shall stand or fall by the Stars and Stripes.

Also, here at the Texel I stay, until I'm ready to leave; that I say in the teeth of Dutchman and Englishman alike."

When this hardy note goes ashore, the Dutch look solemn, Sir Joseph retires with the gout, while the English outside the mouth of the Hel-der, stand oft and on, gnashing their iron teeth.

CHAPTER XIX
NOW FOR THE TRAITOR LANDAIS

While the Dutch and Sir Joseph are debating as to whether Commodore Paul Jones is a rebel, a pirate or a disagreeable guest, that gentleman discovers Landais, with the Alliance, tucked away in a corner of the Texel. Headwinds, and an overplus of English on the high seas, have forced the miscreant into the Helder, and he finds himself as much cooped up as does Commodore Paul Jones. Indeed the miserable Landais is in a far more serious predicament; for, aside from the English outside, waiting at the Helder's mouth like terriers at a rat-hole, the formidable Paul Jones is inside with him, and Landais fears the latter as no Frenchman ever feared the English.

The alarms of Landais are well grounded; Commodore Paul Jones opens negotiations at once. He sends word to Landais to give command of the Alliance to Lieutenant Degge, and at once leave the ship. The word is supplemented by the assurance that at the end of twenty-four hours he, Commodore Paul Jones, shall come aboard the Alliance. Should he then find Landais, he will be put in irons.

"Why not arrest the scoundrel at once?" pleads Lieutenant Dale.

"He is a Frenchman, Dick," returns Commodore Paul Jones, "and I fear to worry Doctor Franklin." Then, assuming a look of cunning, vast and deep: "Wait until my diplomacy unfolds itself. You will find that I have the wisdom of the serpent."

Lieutenant Dale grunts disgustedly. He cares nothing for the wisdom of the serpent, less for any spun-glass diplomacy. What he wants is the Landais blood directly; and says as much.

"Remember," he goes on, "this murderer Landais killed Caswell with that last felon broadside!"

"I shall forget nothing," returns Commodore Paul Jones.

At the end of twenty-four hours, Commodore Paul Jones boards the Alliance. He finds Lieutenant Degge in command; the craven Landais has slipped ashore with all his belongings. Commodore Paul Jones is the last man he cares to face. The latter tells Lieutenant Degge to clap the irons on Landais, should he return, and signal the Serapis.

"You must understand, sir," responds Lieutenant Degge, "that my crew is honeycombed with mutiny. Captain Landais brought about a conspiracy; two-thirds of the ship's company are in it."

"Make me out a list of the leaders, and muster them aft."

Lieutenant Degge gives Commodore Paul Jones the names of twenty. These are called aft—lowering and sullen. Commodore Paul Jones orders them transferred to the Serapis.

"I'll send you an even number to take their places," he says to Lieutenant Degge. "Meanwhile, my old sea-wolves will lick them into patriotic shape. Should they fail, you may find some half dozen of the ringleaders at least, dangling from my yardarms."

The caitiff Landais, driven from his ship, fumes and blusters. He tries to see the French Ambassador, and is refused. Then he sends a challenge to Commodore Paul Jones.

Lieutenant Dale finds the latter mariner in his cabin, blandly triumphant.

"There," he cries, tossing the Landais challenge over to Lieutenant Dale—"there, Dick, read that! You will then see what I meant by telling you to wait until my diplomacy had had time to unfold."

"But you don't mean to fight the creature?" and Lieutenant Dale glances up from his reading, horrified.

"Fight him; and kill him, sir! Why not? Do you suppose for a moment that poor Caswell is to go unavenged?"

"But think what you do! You can't fight this fellow! The man is to be court-martialed."

"Ah, yes, Dick! But observe; I've as yet refrained from making formal charges against him. So far as the books go, he rates as well as you or I."

Commodore Paul Jones gets this off with inexpressible slyness, as one who discloses the very heart of his cunning.

"But my dear Commodore," returns Lieutenant Dale, desperately, "the thing is impossible! This Landais is not a gentleman! He is the commonest of blacklegs."

"Dick! Dick!" remonstrates Commodore Paul Jones; "you do him an injustice! Technically at least you wrong him. You should summon up more fairness. Now, here is how I look at it:" Commodore Paul Jones grows highly judgmatical. "I follow the law, which says that a man is supposed to be innocent until he's shown to be guilty. Influenced by this, which to my mind breathes the very spirit of justice, I make it an unbreakable rule, in matters of the duello, to regard every man as a gentleman unless the contrary has been explicitly demonstrated. No, Dick"—this solemnly—"Landais, whatever you or I may privately think, has still his rights. I shall fight him, Dick."

Commodore Paul Jones sends Lieutenant May-rant ashore, as his representative, to accept the Landais challenge.

"I should have sent you, Dick," he explains to Lieutenant Dale, who inclines to the cloudy because he had been slighted; "but, to tell the truth, I couldn't trust you. Yes; you'd have cut in between us, and fought him in my stead. And the fact is, if you must have it, I've set my heart on killing the rogue myself."

Lieutenant Mayrant finds Landais, vaporing and blustering.

"Pistols; ten paces," says Lieutenant May-rant. "Time and place you may settle for yourself."

"Pistols!" exclaims Landais, his face a muddy gray. Pistols and Paul Jones mean death. With a gesture, as though dismissing an unpleasant thought, he cries: "I shall not fight with pistols! They are not recognized in Prance as the weapons of a gentleman!"

"They are in America," retorts Lieutenant Mayrant. "Neither shall you palter or split hairs! Pistols it shall be; or I tell you frankly that the officers of the Serapis, ay! the very foc'sel hands, will beat you and drub you for a cowardly swab, wherever they come across you."

Landais does not respond directly to this. He walks up and down, stomaching the hard words in silence. For he perceives, as through an open window, that the hidden purpose of Lieutenant Mayrant is to pick a quarrel with him. At last Landais makes it clear that under no compulsion will he fight with pistols. Neither will he give the hopeful Mayrant an opening to edge in a challenge for himself. After a fruitless hour the latter, sad and depressed, returns aboard the Serapis.

"Nothing could have been handled more delicately," he reports to Commodore Paul Jones; "but, do my best, sir, I couldn't coax the rascal to the field."

The next day Lieutenant Dale, making a flimsy excuse about wishing to see the French secretary, goes ashore. He is using a crutch; for, like Lieutenant Mayrant, he was wounded in the battle. He finds the crutch inexpressibly convenient. Having hunted down Landais, whom he finds in a change house, he uses it to belabor that personage, giving him the while such descriptives as "dog!" "spy!" "liar!" "coward!" The heavy Dutchmen, quaffing their beer, interfere to save Landais from the warlike Lieutenant

Dale. That night Landais starts post for Paris, to the mighty disappointment of Commodore Paul Jones.

"You told me you wanted to see the French secretary. It wasn't fair of you, Dick!" is all Commodore Paul Jones says, when he learns of the doings of Lieutenant Dale and his crutch in the change house.

"Well!" grumbles Lieutenant Dale defensively, "so I did want to see the French secretary; although I've now forgotten what it was all about. The sight of that dastard drove it from my head."

The French Ambassador again boards the Serapis. He bears orders from De Sartine, the French Minister of Marine, and a letter from Doctor Franklin, full of suggestions which have the force of orders. The Pallas is a French ship, and the Scarboro captured by it, is a French prize. The Serapis, prize to the Richard, also a French ship, is by the same token a French prize. The French flag must be hoisted on these ships, and the trio made over to the French Ambassador. The Alliance, an American built ship, the King of France doesn't claim. He recommends, however, that it run up French colors, as a diplomatic method of quieting Dutch excitement, which is slowly but surely rising. Doctor Franklin's letter sustains the French claim to the Pallas, the Scarboro and the Serapis. He leaves Commodore Paul Jones to settle flags for the Alliance as he may deem best. The Ambassador makes, in this connection, a second tender of a Captain's commission in the French Navy.

"No," responds Commodore Paul Jones bitterly, "I shall not accept it. King Louis shall have the Serapis, the Pallas and the Scarboro since Doctor Franklin so orders. The Alliance and I, however, shall remain American."

Commodore Paul Jones gives the French Ambassador possession of the Serapis. Also, he waxes sarcastic, and intimates that it is the only way by which the French could have gotten the Serapis into their hands. This piece of wit does him no good, when later he asks it back from De Sartine. Sullen and dogged, he prepares to go aboard the Alliance, and orders the crew of the Serapis to follow.

Again the French Ambassador interferes. What French subjects are on the musters of the Alliance and Serapis must be left in his charge. Commodore Paul Jones is to have none but Americans.

At this some sixty Danes speak up. They may not be Americans, but at least they are not French. Making this announcement, the gallant Scands refuse the orders of the French Ambassador, and pack their kits for the Alliance. These Danes are of the true viking litter, with yellow hair and steel-gray eyes. Their action comes like balm to the sore heart of Commodore Paul Jones. Later when he musters his reorganized crew aboard the Alliance, and makes them a brief talk, he speaks of the desertion of the French. He is interrupted by a youth—small and light and delicate. The youth steps out from among the sailors, and with him come four others. The youth bows half-way to the deck.

"No," he says—"no, Monsieur le Commodore, not all the French have desert. I, Pierre Gerard, am still with you—I, and my four bold comrades, who are brave men."

"They wants to stay, sir," vouchsafes Boatswain Jack Robinson, coming forward to the aid of little Pierre and his companions. "An' so, d'ye see, since I always likes to encourage zeal, I stows 'em away in the long boat till that frog-eatin' Ambassador is over the side. An' so, here they be, game as pebbles, an' a credit to the sta'board watch."

All his prisoners and wounded have been put ashore, under arrangements with the Dutch and the gouty Sir Joseph. Aboard the Alliance, Commodore Paul Jones finds himself at the head of four hundred and twelve war-hardened wolves of the sea, American blood to a man, all save the sixty vikings, and little Pierre with his four.

CHAPTER XX
AIMEE ADELE DE TELISON

It is Christmas day. Out of the furious southwest blows a storm. The English ships, guarding the mouth of the Helder, are driven from their stations, and carried far out to sea. Tired of the Texel, with its French and English and Dutch, Commodore Paul Jones, taking advantage of the English scudding seaward before the gale, runs out with the Alliance, and lays her nose for the English coast, in the very face of the weather.

Being Christmas day, when Commodore Paul Jones puts the Dutch coast astern, there is plum duff and double grog aboard the Alliance. These, and the blue water beneath their fore-foot, mightily cheer the hearts of the crew. The exuberance takes shape in a way grateful to the soul of Commodore Paul Jones. A missive, borne by the tarry hand of Boatswain Jack Robinson, finds him during the larboard watch. As Boatswain Robinson rolls aft, the whole crew follow him, a respectable distance in the rear.

"It's a deppytation," explains Boatswain Robinson, pulling his forelock—"a deppytation of the entire ship's company down to cooks an' cabin-boys, an' be dammed to 'em! They sets forth their views in a round robin, which I hereby tenders."

Boatswain Robinson holds out a square of dingy bown paper. It is signed by every member of the crew, beginning with the redoubtable Robinson. Commodore Paul Jones reads the round robin, which is written in black sprawling characters, while Lieutenant Dale who comes up holds a ship's lantern. Thus runs the document, the compilation whereof has exhausted the forecastle.

"We respectfully request you, sir, to lay us alongside any single-decked English ship to be found in these seas, or any double-decked ship under a fifty."

"My lads," says Commodore Paul Jones, when he finished reading the round robin, "this is what I like. Our ship is a thirty-six, our biggest gun a twelve-pounder. You say 'lay her alongside a fifty gun ship, with her lower tier of eighteen-pounders. I promise that I'll do my best. I'll cruise between St. George's Channel and the Bay of Biscay two full weeks, looking for what you ask. Still, I must tell you that, while I've plenty of hope, I've little expectation. This is winter weather, lads, and the chances of our finding a fight are slim. If we find one, however, I shall, by way of compliment, take you over the Englishman's hammock nettings myself; for I hold you, man and boy, to be as stout a crew as ever primed pistol or laid cutlass to grindstone, and one that it's an honor to lead. Mr. Bo'sen, pipe the men for'ard. Mr. Dale will give orders for another ration of grog all'round. And so, shipmates, I give you a Merry Christmas!"

The Alliance goes looking for a British fifty. But nothing comes of it. Between wind and snow and biting weather, the ships have deserted the open ocean, like wild fowl, for the friendly sheltering warmth of the ports. When the two weeks are up, four weeks more are added to the cruise by common consent. Stores, however, are running low, and following six weeks futile looking about, Commodore Paul Jones stands in for the Isle au Grroaix, and anchors in the harbor of l'Orient.

It is February fourteenth, the day of sweet St. Valentine. Also, it is among the coy and blushing possibilities, that sweet Saint Valentine has been lying in wait for him; for our sailor, home from sea, finds in the hands of his agent a pretty note, which in its sequence is to carry him into the midst of much tenderness and flowery happiness.

The note is from his good friend, the Marchioness de Marsan. The Marchioness asks Commodore Paul Jones, when he is next in l'Orient and can spare himself from his ship, to visit her at her palace. Weary with the sea, sore from the loss of the Serapis, the summons falls in with his tired humor. He leaves the Alliance in charge of Lieutenant Dale, and goes with what haste he may to his friend the Marchioness. That good noblewoman kisses him on both cheeks.

"It is for your victory!" she says. "France is a-quiver with it!"

As Commodore Paul Jones is about to reply, a girl of twenty enters the room.

"Aimee de Telison, Commodore," says the Marchioness, presenting him. Then aside: "She is my ward—my godchild! Is she not beautiful?"

"Beautiful! Skin pink and white! Teeth like pearls or rice! Damask lips, eyes deep and lustrous and large! Hair a flood of red gold! In form a little rounded goddess! Beautiful!"

Thus run the thoughts of the sailor, as the sweetness and witchery of the vision carries his senses along.

"Aimee de Telison!" he repeats in a whisper. "Who is she?"

The Marchioness hesitates; then she returns in the same guarded tones:

"Who is she? She is the daughter of a King."

CHAPTER XXI
ANTONY AND CLEOPATRA

Presently the beautiful Aimee quits the room, and the good Marchioness de Marsan tells her story.

"There is surely no reason why you shouldn't know, my dear Commodore," she says; "since all France knows. Aimee's mother is of the de Tiercelins—a noble house, but impoverished. As a girl the mother was ravishingly lovely. This was in the days of Monsieur le Bel and the Parc-aux-Cerfs. The old king saw Mademoiselle de Tiercelin; the Pompadour did not object. Aimee was born; and presently her mother, whom the king called his 'de Bonneval,' was put away with a pension. The Bonneval's father talked loudly, and was sent to the Bastile as a 'Russian spy.' One may say what one will in the Bastile; the walls are thick and have no ears. The Pompadour looked after poor de Bonneval and the little Aimee. She married the mother to a gentleman named Telison. The Pompadour died; the king died; Aimee was sixteen. Her stepfather de Telison, and her mother de Bonneval neglected her. They said 'She is a Bourbon. Let the Bourbons provide.' So I, who am her godmother, took Aimee. That was four years ago; and now it is as though she were my own child in very fact—I love her so."

"But the present king?"

"Thus far he has done nothing for Aimee. She goes to court; her position is recognized; the king is kind. But you know the cold Savoy blood?—it is stingy! However, that is now of little moment so far as Aimee is concerned, for I am rich."

Commodore Paul Jones is established at the palace of the good Marsan. Sailors are swift to love; the image of Aimee fits into his heart as into a niche that was made for it.

The second day he calls on the Duchess de Chartres—the beautiful girl-Duchess. He wears a guilty feeling at the base of his conscience. Fortunately his cheek is tanned by wind and weather, and the guilty feeling does not show.

The girl-Duchess is with her husband, the Duke de Chartres, who has quit the sea for the shore, his man-of-war for his palace. The girl-Duchess receives Commodore Paul Jones in something of a formal manner, which is a relief to him. His manner is also formal, which is not a relief to her. The Duke, who makes a specialty of democracy, greets him with bluff cordiality as a brother sailor. He congratulates him on beating the "English dogs," whom he hates professionally. Commodore Paul Jones is modest in his replies. For he is not thinking of the Serapis, but on Aimee; and, with the eyes of the girl-Duchess upon him, that guilty feeling overlays all else.

The girl-Duchess watches him through halfshut lids. She almost guesses the truth; for she knows of the good Marsan, and Aimee. Besides, she is a woman, and clairvoyant in matters of the heart.

After an hour with the Duke and the girl-Duchess, Commodore Paul Jones goes back to the good Marchioness de Marsan and to Aimee. As an excuse for his own idleness, he travels down to l'Orient and, albeit the Alliance is as fit as a fiddle, sets Lieutenant Dale, "Dick the practical," to overhauling the ship from truck to keel. Then he returns to the good Marsan and Aimee.

Now he spends sunny hours in the beautiful Aimee's company, and his love creeps and grows upon him like ivy on a wall. The conqueror is conquered; the invincible is overthrown. As for Aimee, her blue eyes become a deeper blue, her pink cheeks take on a warmer pink when he is near. And the good Marsan sees it all, and does not interfere. For she is versed in the world and its ways; and this is France; and after life comes death.

When the ardent sailor would be too ardent, Aimee represses him; the barrier of her modesty is as a barrier of ice between them. Thereupon he loves her the more, and refreshes his soul with Shakespeare:

"Chaste as the icicle

That's curdled by the frost of purest snow,

And hangs on Dian's temple."

Commodore Paul Jones goes down to l'Orient again. Not so much to see after the Alliance, as to pique his love and give it edge. For absence makes the flame burn brighter, and Aimee bursts upon him with a new charm when he has been away.

For all his lovelorn case, however, he makes arrangements for his two pets, Lieutenants May-rant and Fanning, to go privateering for the French, and gives them nearly one hundred and fifty of his fiercest sea-wolves to bear them company.

"Why keep them rusting ashore," says he, "like good blades in their sheaths! No; let the lads sail forth with letters of marque, and make their fortunes."

The Serapis is held by the French as a king's prize, and de Sartine pays Commodore Paul Jones twelve thousand dollars as his share. There are other thousands from other prizes, and, after a French sort, he finds himself rich.

When, following his visit to l'Orient, he returns to the good Marsan, that estimable lady is discovered in a state of much excitement. The Duchess de Chartres has "commanded" the presence of Commodore Paul Jones at her palace.

The prospect does not overcome him. He receives it with steadiness, although privily a-quake because of that feeling of guilt. The good Marsan's excitement is supplanted by wonder to see him take his honors so coolly.

"Ah, these Americans!" she thinks. Then, out loud: "She is a Bourbon, my Commodore! No one below the blood royal has ever received such a summons."

In spite of the uplifted palms of the good Marsan, her "Commodore" refuses to be impressed. He will go; since no one should decline the "command" of royalty. But he will go calmly—hiding of course his sense of guilt, and spreading the skirts of his conscience very wide to hide it.

Aimee hears that he is to go, and cannot avoid a little flutter of alarm. She knows her beautiful kinswoman, the girl-Duchess—knows the spell and the power of her. It gives the tender Aimee a dull ache of the heart. A lone feeling of helplessness overwhelms her, as fears rise up for her poor love that, in so short a space, has become the one sweet thing in life. True, she herself is a Bourbon! But with the bar sinister. How then shall she, obscure and poor and by the left hand, hope to sustain herself in the heart of her lover against the wiles and siren wooings of one who is at once the most legitimate, the most beautiful, and the most wealthy woman in France! The tears gather in the soft eyes.

The good Marsan goes from the room; for she has a deal of sympathy and good sense. Commodore Paul Jones, when now the two are alone, draws Aimee to him, and dries those tears in ways that lovers know. For the first time he folds her in his arms and kisses her lips.

"Perhaps it is also the last time," she thinks sadly.

And the gallant lover, as though he reads her thoughts, kisses her again, and vows by sword and ship to love her always.

Commodore Paul Jones finds the Duchess de Chartres in spirits. She and the Duke give him a suite of apartments that has heretofore been sacred to Bourbon occupation alone. At this the sensation that rocks the Court is profound.

It even reaches the rabbit-faced king—weak rather than dull—at Versailles, and gives him a shock. He draws down the uncertain corners of his undecided mouth, says naught, and goes out under the trees to feed his squirrels. He would be wiser were he to go out into the starved highways and byways of his oppressed realm, and feed his subjects. Did he do so, he might even yet avoid that revolution, which is slowly yet terribly preparing itself in the ante-chamber of Time.

CHAPTER XXII
THE FÊTE OF THE DUCHESS DE CHARTRES

The Duke and Duchess de Chartres give a grand banquet in honor of Commodore Paul Jones. The Duchess asks Doctor Franklin, whom she esteems, and calls "Monsieur le Sage" for his wisdom. Also, to please the worthy doctor, she has Madame de Houdetot, and the rest of his Passy friends, including the vivacious Madame Helvetius.

"Only," says the Duchess, who has weaknesses that favor washtubs—"only I trust that our 'Rich Widow of Passy' will wear a fresh frock, if only to give us something to, talk about."

The good Marsan and Aimee are among the guests. Indeed, it is to see Aimee and Commodore Paul Jones together that has caused the Duchess de Chartres to order the fête. She will bring the pair beneath her eyes—the young Aimee, and the "Commodore," who has become formal. She will then know the best and worst of their hearts.

The Duchess is right in this assumption; for you may no more hide love than smoke. With half-watchfulness, she readily surprises their secret. Still she is gay and light; for her heart is the heart of a Bourbon, and the heart of your Bourbon is never a breakable.

She seats Commodore Paul Jones on her right, which is the thing expected. Aimee is on his other hand; which last excites his suspicions—having that guilty feeling—while attracting the attention of nobody else. Over across is the wise Franklin, who finds himself vastly at home between the Houdetot and the rosy Helvetius, who is a marvel of tidiness.

The Duchess pays a deal of polite attention to Commodore Paul Jones.

"I cannot think, my dear Commodore," she cries, "how, with your ship on fire, and sinking under your feet, you had courage to continue the fight."

"Your royal highness forgets. To surrender would have meant a postponement of the bliss of meeting you."

"Now, Bayard himself," returns the Duchess, "could have said nothing so knightly!"

Aimee glows at this. In the face of her fears, she still likes to hear her lover-hero praised.

"There is a promise!" exclaims the Duchess.

Commodore Paul Jones reddens through the tan. What is coming! There is much of royal recklessness in the Duchess' royal blood; she will now and then say a bold thing.

"You promised," she goes on, "to lay an English frigate at my feet."

Commodore Paul Jones is relieved. More, he is pleased, since the Duchess gives him a chance to be dramatic. He sends for his servant, who brings him a slim morocco case.

"Your royal highness," he says, unbuckling the morocco case; "I shall be better than my word. I lay at your feet, not a frigate truly, but a forty-four gun ship of two decks. Here is the token of it—the sword of as brave a sailor as ever sailed."

Commodore Paul Jones presents the Duchess with the vanquished sword of Captain Pearson, which he has taken from the morocco case. The Duchess, who has not foreseen this return to her sally, is deeply stirred. She receives the sword, and presses the gold scabbard to her lips.

"It is dear to me as the sword of a conquered Englishman!" she cries, turning with swimming eyes upon the company. "It is doubly dear when it comes from my Achilles of the ocean!"

There is a buzz of admiration about the tables. Aimee herself is in a dream of happiness; for she has alarms but no jealousies, and the glory of her lover is her glory.

Before the guests break up for departure, Doctor Franklin and Commodore Paul Jones have a word together.

"I have asked for it," says the Doctor, "and de Sartine leads me to think that, as soon as the ship is refitted, the king will give you the Serapis."

Commodore Paul Jones brightens to a sparkle.

"I could do wonders with so stout a ship," he replies.

"I think you may count on it," goes on the Doctor. "Indeed, when I remember in what manner the French came by the Serapis, I cannot see how the king is to refuse."

"Should I get it, I'll put Dick Dale in command of the Alliance. There shall be no second Landais you may be sure!"

"Speaking of the Alliance," returns the Doctor, "I shall send it to America as soon as the overhaul is finished, with certain munitions of war I've collected."

Commodore Paul Jones' pulse begins to beat uneasily. Antony does not want to leave his Cleopatra. What the Doctor next says, sets him to renewed ease.

"Lieutenant Dale might better take the Alliance across. You will be needed here, if we are to coax the king into giving you the Serapis. There will be time for the Alliance to return before the Serapis is refitted."

Doctor Franklin tells how he has formally relieved Landais from all command, and ordered him to report to the Marine Committee in Philadelphia, on charges of cowardice and treason. Also, Commissioner Arthur Lee has been called home; Congress has become suspicious of his work.

"The man's a greater traitor than Landais!" cries Commodore Paul Jones heatedly.

"Without expressing myself on that point," observes the Doctor, eye a-twinkle, "the situation produced by Mr. Lee's recall, makes another reason why Dale should sail with the Alliance and you stay here. Mr. Lee, I understand, has decided to take passage home in the Alliance."

It is the next day; the Duchess summons Commodore Paul Jones to the morning-room, where she sits alone in the spring sunshine.

"Your love is like your ship, my friend," she observes. "It goes voyaging from heart to heart, as the other does from port to port. No, not a word! I promise that you shall not break my heart. Come, I will show you what makes me safe—safe even from that terrible heart-rover and sea-rover, that buccaneer of the ocean and of love, the invincible Paul Jones."

She smiles; but there is that about the smile which reminds one of the hard glitter of a rapier. She rings a bell, says a low word, and presently a little round-faced boy is brought in. He is the baby son of the Duchess. Commodore Paul Jones has heard of the little boy; but this is his earliest glimpse of him.

He is a handsome child, and Commodore Paul Jones gazes upon him with admiration. The boy is to grow up and, fifty years later, sit on the French throne as the "Citizen King." This, however, is a secret of the future, and neither the mother nor Commodore Paul Jones, as they look on the small, round face, is granted a least glint of it. Released by the nurse, little Louis Philippe toddles across to Commodore Paul Jones, pudgy hands outstretched. The latter catches him up and kisses him. At this the eyes of the Duchess soften with mother-love.

"See!" she remarks, and a sigh and a laugh struggle for precedence on her lips—"See! he is like all of us. He loves you!" She becomes grave. "There is my resource!" she goes on. "My friend, I will let you into a secret. No man's treason, not though he be the bewildering Paul Jones"—this with a tinge of wicked emphasis—"can break a mother's heart. No; she takes refuge in her child, and finds his kisses sweeter than a lover's."

She takes the boy out of his hands, and kisses the little face again and still again. Commodore Paul Jones says no word of protest, explanation or defence. The Duchess is taking her revenge; he knows it, and thinks her entitled to it. Moreover, he is beginning in his own heart to be relieved, and the guilty feeling that gnaws his conscience is sensibly dulled.

The nurse returns and takes the boy. The Duchess gives the little face a last kiss. Then her glance comes back to Commodore Paul Jones.

"Yes, my friend," she says; "love your red-haired Aimee, since you love her; I can give you up; for even though you leave me, you leave me a Bourbon. And yet I feel a small jealousy—just a little stab! For that stab, my friend, you must pay. No one harms a Bourbon, and escapes unpunished." This is said half quizzically, half seriously. "Yes, I shall have my revenge. I intend that you shall marry Aimee."

CHAPTER XXIII
THE WEDDING WITHOUT BELLS

Doctor Franklin journeys down to Lyons, on some secret errand of his own; he will be gone a week. Commodore Paul Jones, at home with the good Marsan, drunk with love, forgets the blue of the ocean in the blue of Aimee's eyes. One sun-filled afternoon he is disturbed by Lieutenant Dale, who stalks in with a scowl on his usually steady face.

"What is it, Dick?" asks Commodore Paul Jones, alive in a moment.

"Something too deep for me, Commodore, or I shouldn't be here with the tangle. Commissioner Lee, with Landais, has taken the Alliance."

"What?"

"It's as I say. Lee declares that Doctor Franklin had no authority to depose Landais. He, Lee, has restored him to command, and the pair have possession of the ship."

"What did you do?"

"I did nothing. I'm a sailor, and pretend to no knowledge of the limits of Mr. Lee's authority. Speaking for myself, I refused to serve with Landais; and Lieutenants Stack, McCarty and Lunt, and Midshipman Lindthwait did the same. We came ashore, and Bo'sen Jack Robinson at the head of sixty of the crew came with us." Commodore Paul Jones, while Lieutenant Dale talks, is thinking. What is to be done! Manifestly nothing. Doctor Franklin is out of reach. Without the Doctor's authority no one can meddle with Arthur Lee, who still has his powers as a commissioner. Besides, there's the Serapis; it is only a question of weeks when he, Commodore Paul Jones, will be given its command. Meanwhile, Lieutenant Dale and the others can disport themselves ashore, as he does. Let Lee and Landais keep the Alliance, since they already have it.

"You've done right, Dick," he says. "Stay ashore then, and keep the lads together; we'll wait for the Serapis. Also, King Louis has given Doctor Franklin the Ariel, a ship-sloop the size of the old Ranger. When I take the Serapis to sea, Dick, you shall sail Captain of the Ariel."

Lieutenant Dale goes his way, and Commodore Paul Jones returns to Aimee, pleased in secret to think he may continue unhindered to sun himself in her smiles. It grinds a bit to think of the "dog Landais," and the "traitor Arthur Lee," in control of the Alliance. Still, all will come right; for is he not to have the Serapis? And while he waits, there is Aimee; and love is even sweeter than war. So he goes back to his goddess, with her deep eyes and red-gold hair, and puts such caitiff creatures as Lee and Landais outside his thoughts. It is for Congress to deal with them.

Commodore Paul Jones is not permitted to forget Lee and Landais. Within the hour, he is again called from the side of Aimee by his friend Genet, a noble upperling in the French foreign office.

"I come to tell you," says Genet, "that Captain Landais and Monsieur Lee have got the Alliance."

"I know!"

"They are to sail in three days."

"Lieutenant Dale has told me."

"He did not tell you that we have issued orders to Thevenard, who commands the forts at the barrier, to sink the Alliance, should she try to put to sea."

"Sink the Alliance!" Commodore Paul Jones is thunderstruck. "My dear Genet, you jest."

"No jest, my friend. The orders have been given. Should the Alliance attempt to pass the harriers, Thevenard will fire on it with all his hundreds of big guns, and snuff it out like a candle. It is by request of your Doctor Franklin."

"Do you tell me that Doctor Franklin asks you to sink the Alliance?"

"He has asked us—for he had some inkling of the designs of Lee and Landais—to prevent them sailing away with the ship. We know of but one way to do that. We must sink it, since we have no ship here to arrest them. So we gave the orders to Thevenard. Those orders, however, we did not impart to Doctor Franklin; and, in good truth, I tell them to you now, not as a French official, but as a friend."

"This must be stopped!" cries Commodore Paul Jones, his habits of decision and iron promptitude reassumed in a moment. "What! Sink two hundred brave, good men, to punish a pair of traitors? Never!"

Genet, who makes a cult of red tape, shrugs his shoulders and spreads his hands.

"It is too late," he says. "There is Doctor Franklin's request. I cannot countermand the orders to Thevenard until he withdraws his request."

"I shall see Thevenard!"

Two hundred and eighty miles in fifty-four hours! An unprecedented thing! And yet Commodore Paul Jones does it, and rides into l'Orient in time to prevail on General Thevenard, who is his friend and his worshipper, to let the Alliance pass free. The forts would else have sunk the ship with their tons upon tons of metal. He saves the Alliance by a narrow margin of hours, and Lee and Landais shake out their sails for America.

"They go to disgrace and grief," thinks Commodore Paul Jones, consoling himself for their escape. Then he considers how he has saved the lives of more than two hundred honest sailors, who have fought well for flag and country, and is consoled in earnest.

Commodore Paul Jones is surrounded by surprises. He is met on the road, while returning to his Aimee, by a message from the Duchess de Chartres.

"Come instantly to me!" it says.

There is a look of mingled sorrow and resentment, with over all a hue of humor, on the Duchess' bright face when she welcomes Commodore Paul Jones.

"The Marchioness de Marsan and I have arranged it," she says, and her glance is wicked and amused.

"Arranged what?"

"Your marriage, my friend! I congratulate you! You and your red-haired, blue-eyed one are to wed."

"With all my heart, then!" says he, turning wicked, too. Manlike, it offends his vanity that one who has pretended to love him so deeply should be now so ready to give him to another. "I could wish no fairer fate."

"But the wedding must be secret."

"Secret! Believe me, I shall tell all France."

"And ruin the blue-eyed one! Hear me, my Commodore—once my beloved, ever to be my friend! I have had a world of trouble in your affairs. I arranged with the Marsan; but only by agreeing that the marriage be buried in secrecy. You know much of the sea; little of the shore when all's said. Should the king hear of Aimee as your wife, he would drive her from court."

"May I ask why!" and his cheek begins to burn angrily.

"You forget that Aimee is a Bourbon," returns the Duchess, with a fashion of malicious satisfaction. He has deserted her for his Aimee; it is her revenge to irritate his pride. "You are a valorous man, and the king makes much of you. Besides, you beat the English, whom he fears and hates. And yet he does not forget that you are a peasant—as I did. Marry Aimee, my friend—. marry a Bourbon, even a Bourbon by the left hand, and King Louis will bolt the doors of France in both your faces. Indeed, the Bastile might be the end of it for your Aimee." "I think your royal highness sees unnecessary ghosts," he replies, with a sneer. Just the same, that linking of the Bastile and Aimee alarms him. "Without pausing to question the king's powers touching Bastiles and French doors, I may tell you he has already heard that I love Aimee. Doctor Franklin, himself, told me." "Love Aimee! Yes; love her as much and to what limit you will! The king will never resent that. But do not let the whisper that you have married Aimee reach the kingly ear. Can you not understand! Here, I will put it in the abstract. A Princess may have a liaison with a peasant, and in the shadow of that dishonor she will remain forever a Princess. Should the Princess, in some gust of virtue, be swept into a marriage with the peasant, she becomes instantly a peasant. It is one of those strange cases, my friend, where the word 'wife' is a stain and the word 'mistress' no stain at all."

It is midnight; two candles burn dimly on the altar of "Our Lady of Loretto." The great chapel is dark and vacant; the feeble light does not reach the vaulted roof, and the groined arches disappear upward in a thick blackness. At the altar stands a priest. Near the rail is gathered a group of four, the Duchess de Chartres, the good Marchioness de Marsan, Aimee— heart a-flutter, her pink cheeks hidden in a veil—and Commodore Paul Jones. The priest draws the Duchess aside.

"Your royal highness," he whispers, pleadingly, "I am afraid."

"Afraid of whom, pray?"

"The king, your royal highness."

The Duchess makes an angry motion with her hand, while her little boot smites the stone floor and sends an echo through the room's vast emptiness.

"Father Joseph, observe! You are my almoner. Through your hands I give fifty thousand louis to the poor of Paris, and keep you in fatness besides. It is I, not the king, whom you should fear." And so, before the flickering altar candles, Commodore Paul Jones weds Aimee Adele de Telison. In the book which the Duchess and the good Marsan sign as witnesses, Father Joseph, with a pen that shakes a little, records the nuptials of "Monsieur le Joignes and Mademoiselle Adele de Bonneval." For "de Bonneval" was the dead King's name for Aimee's mother in the days of Monsieur le Bel and the Parc-aux-Cerfs.

CHAPTER XXIV
THAT HONEYMOON SUB ROSA

The Duchess kisses Aimee, and the good Marsan drives back to her palace with the blissful ones through the black midnight Paris streets. Commodore Paul Jones is in a trance of happiness. Aimee creeps into his arms and whispers "Mon Paul," and the surrender of the Serapis is forgotten, as a thing trivial and transient, in the surrender of this girl with the glorious red-gold hair.

Summer runs away into autumn, and the brown tints of October show in the trees. The honeymoon has been one of secrecies and subterfuges, and perhaps the tenderer and sweeter because sub rosa. Commodore Paul Jones tears himself now and again from Aimee's arms to urge the business of the Serapis. He is seconded by Aimee, to whom his glory is as dear as his love.

Doctor Franklin tells the king that he should give Commodore Paul Jones the ship, and is referred to de Sartine. The oily minister slips away from the proposal, and the king sends Commodore Paul Jones a "Sword of Honor" and the title of "Chevalier." The impatient sailor bites his lip, and gives the plaything sword to Aimee.

"I asked for a ship, not a sword," says he. "As for 'Chevalier,' since I'm already a Commodore, it looks like promotion down-hill."

"The king," explains Doctor Franklin, "does not, I fear, forgive your refusal of his captain's commission when you lay at the Texel."

"And I," he returns, "continue to regard that offer of a commission as a piece of royal impertinence."

Commodore Paul Jones determines to bring the king to a decision. He walks in the royal gardens with his ally, Genet, and comes upon the king feeding his interminable squirrels. The king—for democracy is becoming a fashion—greets Commodore Paul Jones with outstretched hands.

"But do not tell me," concludes the king, "that you come for a ship."

"It is to ask for the Serapis, sire."

The poor king rubs his head, his vague lip twitches, while the unlocked jaw multiplies the feebleness of his weak face.

"Chevalier, I cannot," he returns. In a tone of pathos, he continues: "Congratulate yourself, my friend, that you are not a king. You would be compelled to have ministers, and they would make a slave of you—as they have of me."

"It is over," says Commodore Paul Jones, to Doctor Franklin. "There is no hope of the Serapis."

"Take the Ariel, then, and return to Philadelphia," replies the Doctor. "There is the America, seventy-four guns, building on the Portsmouth stocks. I've written the Marine Committee to give you that."

Commodore Paul Jones holds Aimee close. He kisses her dear lips. "In the spring I shall return, my love," he promises. "Three little months, and you are in my arms again."

Aimee whispers something, and then buries her face in his breast. The blush she is trying to hide spreads and spreads until it covers the back of the fair neck, and the red of it is lost in the roots of the red-gold hair.

"Good!" he cries in a burst of joy, holding her closer. "Good! Now I shall have something to dream of and return to."

It is a raw, flawy February day when Commodore Paul Jones lands in Philadelphia. Arthur Lee, with his poisonous mendacities, has preceded him. He is called before the Marine Committee, to reply to a list of questions, that in miserable effect amount to charges. Anger eating his heart like fire, he answers the questions, and is then voted a resolution of thanks and confidence.

Knowing no other way, he seeks a quarrel with Arthur Lee, the fiery, faithful Cadwalader at his elbow. Mad Anthony Wayne, acting for him, meets Arthur Lee informally. The latter does not like the outlook.

"Who is he?" exclaims Arthur Lee, inventing a defensive sneer. "Either the son of a Scotch peasant or worse, and a man who has changed his name. By what right does such a person demand satisfaction of a gentleman!"

"Permit me to suggest," returns Mad Anthony, beginning to bristle, "that I shall regard a refusal to fight, based on the ground you state, as a personal affront to myself. More; let me tell you, sir, that he who shall seek to bar Paul Jones from his plain rights, on an argument aimed at his gentility, will get nothing by his pains but the name of coward."

"You think so!" responds Arthur Lee, his sneer somewhat in eclipse at the stark directness of Mad Anthony.

"I know so, sir. When you speak of Paul Jones, you speak of the conqueror of the Drake and the Serapis. Also, when you deal with me, you deal with one who is the equal of any Lee of your family, sir."

Mad Anthony blows through his warlike nose ferociously, and Arthur Lee is silent. Meanwhile, the excellent Cadwalader, ever painstaking in matters of bloodshed, prepares a challenge, which he intends shall be a model for succeeding ages, when studying the literature of the duello.

It is at this pinch that the peace-loving Morris, helpless and a bit desperate, brings the weight of General Washington to bear upon the combative one. The "Father of his Country" succeeds where Mr. Morris has failed, and silences all talk of a duel. As a reward for that gentleman's eleventh-hour docility, he prevails upon Congress to give Commodore Paul Jones command of the half-built America, in accord with the request of Doctor Franklin, already in its dilatory hands.

Commodore Paul Jones goes to Portsmouth to oversee the launching and the equipment of his new seventy-four. Disappointment dogs him; for Lord Cornwallis surrenders, and Congress, in a fit of foolish generosity, presents the America to France, as a slight expression of its thanks for the part she played in the capture of that English nobleman. Commodore Paul Jones sees his just-completed seventy-four, over which he has toiled like a poet over his verse, and wherein he was to presently sail away to conquer fresh honors for himself and his Aimee, hoist the French flag and receive a French captain on its quarter-deck. Steadying himself under the blow, with a grim philosophy which he has begun to cultivate, he goes back to Philadelphia. He finds letters from France awaiting him; one is from his Aimee, written in a tremulous, wavering hand. It must have borne wonderful news, for in his reply he says:

"Present my compliments to your sister. Tell her to exert her tenderest care toward you and her sweet little godson. Also cover him with kisses from me."

CHAPTER XXV
CATHERINE OF RUSSIA

Commodore Paul Jones, nervously irritable with the loss of the America, asks leave of Congress to go as a volunteer with the French fleet, which hopes to find and fight the English in the West Indies. Congress consents, and he sails southward with Captain Vaudreuil, to fight yellow fever, not English, and return much shaken in health. As a solace and a recuperative, he sends divers cargoes of oil to Europe on a speculation, and makes forty thousand dollars. All the time he is pining to get back to Paris, his Aimee, the good Marsan, as well as Aimee's sister's "sweet little godson," that must "be covered with kisses." He is detained by his accounts with the government and his claims for prize money. After heart-breaking delays, his affairs are adjusted; again he finds himself outward bound for France. His Aimee meets him with kisses sweet as heaven. He unlocks her white arms from his neck, and asks in a whisper:

"Where is he?"

"He is dead!" she says, with a rush of tears.

Then she carries him to a quiet cemetery, and, taking his hand, leads him to a little grave, upon which the new grass has not grown two weeks. There is a tiny headstone of pale granite, and on it the one word:

"Paul."

His gaze is long and steadfast as he holds fast by his Aimee's hand. Then his tears are united with hers; they stand bowed above the little grave.

Commodore Paul Jones and his Aimee, while ever together, formally conceal the tie that binds them. He has business with the king about prize money; she has petitions before the king about the blood that is common to her veins and his; and both the good Marsan and Doctor Franklin say it is better that the king should not know. And so the king goes feeding his squirrels and forgetting his people, in ignorance of what took place on that midnight before the candle-lighted altar of Our Lady of Loretto. But the wise old world is not so thick, and winks and smiles and wags its wise old head; and whenever it passes a pretty cottage in the Rue Vivienne it points and whispers tolerantly. For the wise old world loves lovers; and because Aimee always officially resides with the good Marsan when her "Paul" is in Paris, and actually resides with that amiable gentlewoman when her "Paul" is in London, or Copenhagen, or elsewhere on the complex business of those prize moneys, no one finds fault. And so four years of love and truth and sweetness, four beautiful years, throughout which the birds sing and the sun shines always, come and go for Commodore Paul Jones and his Aimee; and every noble door in France swings open at their approach.

The prize money gets into a tangle, and Commodore Paul Jones consults his friends, Mirabeau and the venerable Malesherbes. Then he visits America, and is feted and feasted, while his Aimee—each year rounder and plumper and more bewitching—with the red-gold hair growing ever redder and more golden—stays in Paris by the side of the good Marsan, and keeps a loving eye on the vine-clothed cottage in the Rue Vivienne.

Nothing can exceed the honors wherewith Commodore Paul Jones is stormed upon and pelted while in America. He is banqueted by the Morrises, the Livingstons, the Hamiltons, the Jays, while—what is more to his heart's comfort—he is visited by Dale and Fanning and Mayrant and Lunt and Stack and Potter and scores of his old sea wolves of the Ranger and Richard, who crowd round him to press his hand. In the end he drinks a last cup of wine at the Livingston Manor House, rides down to the foot of Cortlandt Street, and goes aboard the Governor Clinton, which, anchors hove short, awaits him. It is his last glass in America, his last glimpse of the shores for which he fought so valorously; November sees him in the Straits of Dover, nineteen days, out from Sandy Hook.

He goes to Paris, and the king has him to lunch at Versailles—a nine-days' social wonder, the like of which has not been witnessed by a staring world since an elder Louis dined Jean Bart. The royal luncheon over, Commodore Paul Jones again settles down to the dear smiles and the love of his Aimee, while the aristocracy of France lionizes the one and worships the other.

One day Mr. Jefferson, now America's Minister to Versailles, and greatly the friend of our two love birds, walks in upon them in that little vine-embowered cottage in the Rue Vivienne. He has big news. The Empress Catherine asks Commodore Paul Jones to become an admiral in the Russian navy. The Turks are troubling her; she wants him to sweep these turbaned pests from the Black Sea.

The cheek of Commodore Paul Jones flushes, his eye lights up. Between love and war his heart was formed to swing like a pendulum. Now he has loved for a season, he would like nothing better than another game with those "iron dice of destiny," vide licet cannon balls; and where should be found a fitter table than the Black Sea, or a more eligible adversary than the Turk? Thus it befalls that his Aimee goes to court with Madam Campan, the noble daughter of the noble Genet, and translates English plays into French for the amusement of Versailles; while be, hot of heart and high of head, as one who snuffeth the battle afar off, makes a straight wake for St. Petersburg.

Commodore Paul Jones meets the Empress Catherine in her Palace of Czarsko-Selo. Outside the snow lies thick; for it is April, and winter is ever reluctant to quit St. Petersburg. He is pricked of curiosity concerning this Russian Empress, for whom he is to draw his sword. He hopes—somewhat against hope, it is true, when he recalls her sixty years—that she will prove beautiful. For he is so much the knight of romance that he fights with more pleasure for a pretty face than for a plain one.

The Empress is before him; he can now put his hopes to the test. His eyes fall upon a thick, gross figure—a woman the antithesis of romance.

Her mouth is coarse, her nose high and hawkish, her forehead full, her gaze hard and level, her whole face harsh—having been so often burned and swept of passion. And yet he feels the power of this white, fire-eyed savage, with her heart of a Phryne and her brain of a Henry the Eighth. There is so much that is palpable and brutish about her, however, that he stands off from her contact and remembers with regret his delicate Aimee of the red-gold locks.

Commodore Paul Jones has been too well trained as a courtier to let fall the polite mask which he wears, and nothing could be more elaborately suave than are the manners he assumes. The ferocious Catherine gets some glimmer of his inward thought for all that. Every inch the Empress, she is even more the woman. To the day of her death the unpardonable offence in any male of her species is a failure to fall in love with her. She receives some chilling touch of her new Admiral's aversion, and it turns her into angry ice. Still, if he will not sigh for her, he shall serve her: so she says to herself. He remains in St.

Petersburg a fortnight; the Empress sees him more than once. When they are together, they talk of Potemkin, Suwarrow, the Turks, and the Black Sea.

CHAPTER XXVI
AN ADMIRAL OF RUSSIA

Admiral Paul Jones travels to the mouth of the Dnieper and joins Potemkin, who is a military fool. Suwarrow, old and cunning and vigilant and war-wise, is another man. He goes aboard his flagship, the Vladimir, of seventy guns. From the beginning he is befriended by the grizzled Suwarrow and thwarted by the foppish Potemkin. This latter is a discarded favorite of Catherine; and, since she is very loyal to a favorite out of favor, he knows he may take liberties. Old Suwarrow, over his brandy, tells Potemkin's story to Admiral Paul Jones.

"He kept the Empress' smiles for a season," explains Suwarrow; "when all of a sudden, having seen Moimonoff, she fills Potemkin's pockets with gold and jewels, gives him a two-thousand-serf estate, and bids him 'travel,' as she bid twenty of his predecessors travel. 'In what have I offended?' whines Potemkin. 'In nothing,' returns the Empress. 'I liked you yesterday; I don't like you to-day; that is all. So you see, my friend, that you can no longer stay in Petersburg, but must travel!' This was ten years ago," continues old Suwarrow. "Potemkin comes down here, and the Empress puts him in charge, and sustains him in all he says and does. My dear Admiral, you must get along with Potemkin to get along with her."

Admiral Paul Jones is by no means sure that he must get along with Potemkin, and regrets that he quitted France, which holds his Aimee. However, being aboard the Vladimir, and having to his signal twenty ships, he resolves to strike one blow for the savage Catherine, if only to see how a Russian fights and what battering a Turk can stand. It will give him something to talk of, something by which he may compare the English and French and Americans, when next at his ease, with Genet or Jefferson or mayhap King Louis as a fellow conversationist.

The chance comes; Admiral Jones engages the Turkish fleet off Kinburn Head, and destroys it after sixteen hours' fighting—sinking some, burning others, breaking completely the power of the Crescent. The Turks bear a loss of twenty-nine ships and more than three thousand sailors, while Admiral Paul Jones loses but three small ships. Having advantage of the victory, old Suwarrow brings his army across the Boug. At one blow, Admiral Paul Jones unlocks the Liman and throws it open to the victorious entrance of old Suwarrow.

Oczakoff falls; Admiral Paul Jones, sick of the cowardice and duplicity of Potemkin and his parasite Nassau-Siegen, relinquishes his command. He bids old Suwarrow good-bye, and travels in a manner of lordly leisure, not at all Russian, but particularly American, back to St. Petersburg and the Empress. As he bids farewell to old Suwarrow, the latter detains him:

"Wait!" Then he takes from one of his camp chests a priceless cloak of sea-otter and sable, lined with yellow silk, and an ermine jacket, white as snow, set off with heavy gold frogs. "Take them, mon Paul," says the old soldier, pressing them upon Admiral Paul Jones. "They are too fine for me." Here he looks complacently at his threadbare gray coat and muddy boots. "No; were I to wear such feathers, my soldiers, who are my children, wouldn't know their old papa Suwarrow." The Empress receives Admiral Paul Jones in her palace of the Hermitage. She is affable, condescending, appreciative, and assigns him to command the naval forces in the Baltic. She makes him rich in gold; for, while the Empress will so far humor Potemkin as to remove Admiral Paul Jones out of his way, she will not fail of doubly rewarding that mariner for the victory which Potemkin is now trying to steal. Admiral Paul Jones grows dissatisfied, however. The Russian nobility intrigues against him, and de Segur, the French Minister, must come to his rescue. They steal his letters from Aimee; and, not hearing from his beloved, he becomes homesick. He tells the Empress that he must go; she consents when he promises to continue drawing full pay as Admiral. That agreed to, she allows him leave of absence for two years, and back he goes to Paris and his Aimee's arms. He calls on De Segur, the French Minister, before he starts, and thanks him for his friendship. "But you will return?" says De Segur. "Never! I want no more of Russia and its Russians! What is this Court of Catherine, but a place where vilest purposes are arrived at by agencies most wretched, and artifices that should disgrace a dog? I am of an honor unfit for such a place, as silk is unfit for mire. The very people are without charity or a commonest humanity. They are like the wolves of their own forests; should they discover one of their brothers, wounded or stricken down, instead of offering aid, they would fall upon him—rending and devouring him!"

"Sixteen long months! Sixteen dreary months you have been gone!" says Aimee, when they are again together at the cottage in the Rue Vivienne.

"They are over, little one," he replies, "over, never to return. Aside from being separated from you, which is to be separated from the sun" —here he caresses her red-gold hair—"they were the sixteen months most miserable of my life."

CHAPTER XXVII
THE HOUSE IN THE RUE TOURNON

And now dawn many days of love and peace and plenty for Admiral Panl Jones, days in the midst of friends, glad days made sumptuous by a beautiful woman, who is a king's daughter crowned with a wealth of red-gold hair. He has his business, too, and embarks in speculation; wherein he shows himself as much a sailor of finance as of the sea. The imperial Catherine refuses to lose him; but pays to the last like an Empress, bidding him prolong his vacation while he will. He grows rich. He has twelve thousand pounds in the bank; while in America, Holland, Denmark, Belgium and England his interests flourish. He sells his plantation by the Rappahannock for twenty-five hundred dollars—less than a dollar an acre; for he says that he has no more heart to own slaves, and the plantation cannot be worked without them.

The little happy cottage in the Rue Vivienne grows small; neither is it magnificent enough for his Aimee, of whom each day he grows more proud and fond. So he removes, bag and baggage, to a mansion in the Rue Tournon. There the rooms are grand, ceilings tall, fireplaces hospitably wide.

The wide fireplaces will do for winter; just now he swings a hammock in the back garden, which is thick-sown of trees and made pleasant by a plushy green May carpet of grass. Here he lolls and reads and receives his friends. For the careful Aimee counsels rest, and much staying at home; because he is a long shot from a hale man, having been broken with that fever in the West Indies, and in no wise restored by the mists and the miasmas of the Dnieper marshes.

Through the summer the back garden is filled with chairs, and the chairs are filled by friends. In the autumn, and later when winter descends with its frosts, the chairs and the incumbent friends gather in a semicircle about the wide flame-filled crackling fireplaces. There be times when the wine passes; and the freighted mahogany sideboards discover that they have destinies beyond the ornamental.

French politics bubbles and then boils; Paris is split by faction. Mirabeau controls the Assembly; Lafayette has the army under his hand—a weak, vacillating hand! These two are of the Moderates.

Admiral Paul Jones, coolly neutral in what sentiments go shaking the hour, has admirers in the parties. They come to him, and talk with him, and drink his wines in the shade of the back garden, or by the opulent fireplaces. Robespierre and Danton, as well as Mirabeau and Lafayette, are there. Also, Bertrand Barère, who boasts that he is not French but Iberian, one whose forbears came in with Hannibal. Later, Barère will preach an open-air sermon on the "Life and Deeds of Admiral Paul Jones." Just now in the Assembly he makes ferocious speeches, garnished of savage expletives culled from the language of the Basques.

Warmest among friends of Admiral Paul Jones is the Thetford corset-maker Tom Paine, with his encarmined nose and love of freedom. Also Gouverneur Morris, who has succeeded Mr. Jefferson as America's Minister in France, comes often to the Rue Tournon. The pair are with him every day; and because all three like politics, and no two of them share the same views, dispute is deep. Aimee of the red-gold hair takes no part in these discussions, but sits watching her "Paul" with eyes of adoration, directing the servants, with a motion of the hand, to have a care that the debaters do not voice their beliefs over empty glasses.

Admiral Paul Jones, while a republican, gives his sympathies to the king, in whom there is much weakness, but no evil.

"They must not kill the king!" says he.

"And why not?" demands Tom Paine, whose bosom distills bitterness, and who holds there are no good kings save dead kings. "Has France no Cromwell? We are both born Englishmen, Paul; our own people ere this have killed a king."

"Tom," cries Admiral Paul Jones, heatedly,

"Cromwell and England should not be cited as precedents here. King Louis is no Charles; and, as for Cromwell, there isn't the raw material in all France to make a Cromwell."

Gouverneur Morris says nothing, but sips his wine; remembering that, as the minister of a foreign nation, he should bear no part in French politics.

The Parisian rabble insult the king, and Lafayette, in command of the military about the Tuileries, sadly lacks decision. Then comes the "Day of Daggers;" the poor king, advised by the irresolute Lafayette, yields to the mob, and the assembled notables are disarmed. The anger of Admiral Paul Jones is extreme. He breaks forth to his friend Tom Paine:

"Up to this time I've been able to find reasons for the king's gentleness; but to-day's action was not gentle, it was weak. I pity the man—beset as he is by situations to which he is unequal. Lafayette cannot long restrain the sinister forces that confront him. He has neither the head nor the heart nor the hand for it. This is a time for grapeshot. I only wish that I might be in command of those thirty cannon parked about the palace, and have with me, even for a day, my old war-dogs of the Ranger and the Richard. Believe me, I should offer the mob convincing reasons in support of conservatism and justice; I should teach it forbearance at the muzzles of my guns."

"But the rabble might in its turn teach you," retorts Tom Paine, with a republican grin.

"Bah!" he exclaims, snapping contemptuous fingers. "They of the mob are but sheep masquerading as tigers. One whiff of grapeshot, and they would disappear." Then he continues, thoughtfully: "Their saddest trait is their levity. They are ridiculous even in their patriotism. Their emblems, representative of the grand sentiments they profess, are as childish as the language in which they proclaim them is fantastic. There is the red cap! Borrowed from the gutters, they make it the symbol of sovereignty! As though a ship were better for being keel up."

Mirabeau, with his lion's face, comes in. He is in a fury, and declares that Lafayette is a practising hypocrite in his pretences of attachment to the king.

"Hypocrisy!" cries Mirabeau. "That, at least, is a lesson in the school of liberty he never learned from Washington."

Others of the Moderates arrive, and join in the conversation.

"You must understand, gentlemen," observes Admiral Paul Jones warmly, "that I, in my time, have fought eight years for liberty. But I did not fight with the decrees of blood-mad Assemblies, or the plots of secret clubs."

Those present smile tolerantly; for the mighty Paul is a person of many privileges, the one man in France who may speak his mind.

"You do not deeply respect the Assembly?" remarks Mirabeau, with a sour smile.

"The Assembly? What is it? A few who talk all the time, and a great many who applaud or hiss! Everything about it is theatrical. It struggles for epigram not principle, and the members would sooner say a smart thing than save France."

Paris is turmoil and uproar and tumult. To keep his mind from that strife which surrounds him, and into which he longs to plunge, Admiral Paul Jones puts in hours with his secretary, Benoît-André, dictating his journals. Also, business calls him to London, where he is much celebrated by the Whigs. He hobnobs with Fox and Sheridan, while Walpole carries him away to Strawberry Hill. He is with Walpole, when word arrives that Mirabeau is dead.

"What will be the effect in Paris'?" asks Walpole.

"What will be the effect! It will unchain the worst elements. The Assembly will now go to every red extreme. While Mirabeau lived, that strange concourse of evil spirits had a master. He is gone; the animals are without a keeper."

Admiral Paul Jones returns to Paris, and finds a letter from Mr. Jefferson, now Secretary of State. Mr. Jefferson asks him to discover how far Europe will co-operate to crush out piracy in the Mediterranean. Also, he explains that President Washington will want the services of Admiral Paul Jones when he sends an expedition against the Barbary States.

While he is reading Mr. Jefferson's letter, a deputation from the Assembly waits on him, and sets forth informally that it is the present French purpose to reorganize the navy, and call him, Admiral Paul Jones, to the command.

"Would you accept?" asks the deputation.

"It would be, gentlemen," he returns, "the part of prudence, and I think of modesty, to defer crossing that bridge till I come to it."

When the deputation goes away, he calls Benoît-André, and sits long into the night dictating a treatise on reforming the French navy. He points out how its present inefficiency arises from the fact that, for centuries, it has been the feeding-ground of a voracious but incompetent aristocracy, a mere asylum for impoverished second sons, and other noble incapables. He sends a copy of his treatise to Walpole, who writes him a letter.

"My dear Admiral," says he of Strawberry Hill; "let France go. Either return home to America and rest upon your laurels, or come over to England, where even those who do not love you admire you. You have fought under two flags; isn't that enough? I take your pamphlet to be simply a bid for a commission in the new French navy, and, because I love and admire you, I hope it will fail. It will be better so. Your laurels, won off Flamboro' Head, will else be turned to cypress, when, as a French admiral, you become the target of British broadsides, with none of your stout Yankee tars to stand by and man your guns."

The winter is at an end; the grass of spring is starting. Admiral Paul Jones receives a letter from President Washington, who speaks of the Barbary States, and asks him to give up his commission in the Russian service. There have been two whose requests with him were ever final—Franklin and Washington. He does not hesitate, but forwards his resignation to Catherine. She will not accept, and puts forward old Suwarrow.

"Do not, my good brother," writes the old soldier—"do not let any siren entice you from the service of the Empress. Your Frenchmen are preparing a stew of mischief that must soon keep all Western Europe busy to save themselves. That will be Russia's time. We shall then have a free hand with the Turk. Our command of the Black Sea is safe. Since you were there, we have built nine new ships of the line, and six stout frigates. You shall have them all. Also, I can now protect you from Court intrigues, which I could not do before. Courtiers, since Ismail, no longer trouble me; I brush them away like flies. In a new Turkish campaign, I would be Generalissimo by land and sea; you would be responsible to no one but me—a situation which, I flatter myself, would not be intolerable to you. Now, my good brother, the Empress has a copy of this letter, and agrees with all I say. Make no entanglements in the west; return to your old papa Suwarrow as soon as you can, and we shall discuss plans."

Old Suwarrow's missive fails of its hoped-for effect. Admiral Paul Jones gets out President Washington's letter and reads it again. Then he sends a polite but peremptory resignation to Catherine, and ends forever with the Russians.

"But, mon Paul," says Aimee, who looks over his shoulder, "what a compliment! England, France, Russia, America—the whole world calls you! And the answer to all"—here a kiss—"is that you shall stay with your Aimee until she coaxes back your health."

CHAPTER XXVIII
LOVE AND THOSE LAST DAYS

Aimee is right. Admiral Paul Jones, never his old sound self since that last cruise in the West Indies, is ill. Gourgaud says it is his lungs, and commands him to take care of himself. He obeys by sticking close to the red-gold Aimee, and the pleasant house in the Rue Tournon, with its fireplaces in the winter and its tree-shaded back garden in the summer—summer, when the hammock is swung.

Now a stream of visitors pours in upon him. Even the poor king, in the midst of his troubles, sends to ask after the health of the "Chevalier Jones." At odd hours, when visitors do not overrun him, he dictates his journals to Benoît-Andre, while Aimee gently swings his hammock with her white hand.

The girl with the red-gold hair.

It is a hazy July day; the drone of pillaging bees, busy among the flowers, fills the back garden in the Rue Tournon. It is one of Admiral Paul Jones' "good days;" a-swing in his hammock, he chats with Major Beaupoil about a recent dinner at which he was the guest of Jacobin honor.

"It was at the Cafe Timon," he says, "a favorite rendezvous of the Jacobins. Believe me, Major, while I cannot speak in highest terms of the Jacobins, I can of the Cafe Timon. One day I hope to take you there."

Gouverneur Morris is announced. He tells Admiral Paul Jones of advices from Mr. Jefferson, and that Mr. Pinckney has been selected Minister to St. James.

"What, to my mind," concludes Mr. Morris, "is of most consequence, Mr. Pinckney bears with him from President Washington your commission as an Admiral in the American navy. You are to be ready, you note, to sail against those Barbary robbers when the squadron arrives."

"I shall not alone be ready," he returns, "I shall be delighted." He springs from the hammock, and takes a quick turn up and down the garden. The prospect of a brush with the swarthy freebooters of the Mediterranean animates him mightily.

Other visitors are announced. Barère, Lafayette, Carnot, Cambon, Vergniaud, Marron, Collot, Billaud, Kersaint, Gensonne, Barbaroux and Louvet one after the other arrive. Laughter and jest and conversation become the order of the afternoon; for all are glad, and argue, from his high spirits, the soon return to health of Admiral Paul Jones. There has been no more cheerful hour in the Rue Tournon back garden. Corks are drawn and glasses clink.

The talk leaves politics for religion. "My church," observes Admiral Paul Jones—"my church has been the ocean, my preacher the North Star, my choir the winds singing in the ship's rigging."

"And your faith?" asks Major Beaupoil.

"You may find it, my dear Major, in Pope's Universal Prayer:

'Teach me to feel another's woe,

To hide the faults I see;

That mercy I to others show,

Such mercy show to me.'

"There!" he concludes, "I call that stanza a complete boxing of the religious compass."

Gourgaud looks in professionally, and is inclined to take a solemn view of his patient's health. He rebukes him for running about the garden among his guests.

"You should not have permitted it," says Gourgaud, admonishing Aimee with upraised finger.

"But he refused to be restrained!" returns Aimee, ruefully.

"Gourgaud!" the patient breaks forth cheerily, "you know the aphorism: At forty every man is either a fool or a doctor. Now I am over forty; and, as a fellow-practitioner, I promise you that our patient, Paul Jones, is out of danger and on the mend." Then, gayly: "Come, Gourgaud, don't croak! Take a glass of wine, man; you frighten Aimee with your long looks." Gourgaud takes his wine; but his looks are quite as long as before.

Abruptly and apropos of nothing, Admiral Paul Jones decides to make his will.

"Your will!" protests Gouverneur Morris, somewhat aghast. "But you haven't been in such health for months."

"Not on account of my health," he explains, "but because of those Barbary pirates."

Notaries are brought in by Benoît-André, and the will is drawn. The gallant testator is for giving all to his Aimee.

"The house you already have," says he; "and also an annuity. Now I leave you the rest; and Beaupoil shall be executor, with Morris as a witness. There; it is arranged!"

But it is not arranged. The red-gold Aimee points out that he has certain nieces and nephews in Scotland and Virginia; they must not be forgotten. He yields to amendments in behalf of those nieces and nephews. Then the will is sealed and signed.

"It has eased my mind," he says, giving the document into the hands of Major Beaupoil for safe-keeping—"it has eased my mind more than I supposed possible." Then, with a look at Aimee: "There will be enough, petite, to take care of you, even though our friends here turn the country bottom-side up. Luckily, too, the property is in England and America and Holland, where values stand more steadily than they do in France."

Aimee remembers the "Sword of Honor," given by King Louis for that victory over the Serapis.

"You always declared it should go to your friend, Dale," she says.

"So I do still!"

Aimee brings the sword. She presses the gilt scabbard to her lips; then she puts it in the hands of her "Paul." He half draws the blade, and considers it with an eye of pride.

"You see this sword?" he remarks to Gouverneur Morris, "Should I die, carry it with my love to Dick Dale—my good old Dick, who did more than any other man to help me win it!"

It is nine o'clock; night has fallen. The many friends have gone their homeward ways. The back parlor of the house in the Rue Tournon is peaceful and still.

Admiral Paul Jones sits in his cushioned easy-chair reading a volume of Voltaire. Now and then he addresses to Aimee some comment of agreement or disagreement with his lively author. Aimee offers no counter comments, but smiles accord to everything; for her heart is lighter and her bosom more tranquil than for many a day, as she basks in the sunshine of new hopes for the restoration of her "Paul."

Some duty of the house calls Aimee. She leaves her Paul the lamplight shining on the pages of the book, his loved face in the shadow. She pauses at the door, her deep, soft eyes full of worship.

Aimee is on the stair returning. An ominous sound reaches her ears! Her heart grows cold; alarm seizes her by the throat, as though a hand clutched her! She knows by some instinct that the end has come, and her "Paul" lies dead or dying! She can neither move nor cry out!

Presently she regains command of herself. With quaking limbs she mounts the stair. The door of the back drawing-room stands open. The lamp still burns, but its radiance no longer lights the pages of the philosopher of Fernay. They fall across the motionless body of her "Paul." He lies with head and shoulder resting on a couch, which he was trying to reach when stricken down.

Aimee gazes for one horror-frozen moment. Then, with a wailing sob, as from the depths of her soul, she throws her arms about him. She covers the marble lips with kisses—those dauntless, defiant lips!—while her thick hair, breaking from its combs, hides, as with a veil of red and gold, the loved face from the prying lamp.

Napoleon is reading those gloomy despatches which tell of Trafalgar. Crushing the paper in his hand, he paces the floor, his pale, moody face swept by gusty emotions of pain and anger and disappointment.

"Berthier, how old was Paul Jones when he died?"

"Forty-five, sire."

There comes a gloom-filled silence; the gray, brooding eyes seek the floor in thought. Then the pacing to and fro is resumed, that hateful despatch still clutched fast in the nervous fingers.

"Berthier: Paul Jones did not fulfil his destiny."

THE END